Dear Melanie,
Thank you all so
truly one an amazi[ng]
words on these pag[es]
follow Isaac's journ[ey.]

Natasha

WHAT ISAAC LEARNED

"To my son Isaac…Should life ever leave you hopeless and alone, may the words on these pages show you how to move on because life is precious. You need only to learn how to walk the path you chose…"

                                        Love, Mom

PROLOGUE

Stop and take a moment to look around you. For every man, woman and child you see, there was someone in their life that did something remarkable so that they could live. How then, do you thank someone who has given up everything so that you could live?

Six months have passed since three lives were saved in exchange for one sacrifice. Two weeks ago, I watched movers cover the furniture in bubble wrap and bury every piece of clothing into boxes- all to be stored or given away. Their efficiency made me angry as they handled his things without thought or care. Did they not know these once belonged to a great man?

But I eventually reminded myself they were simply doing their job. For them, it was all the same because they had never met him. They didn't know that the shirts had to be folded a certain way; and the dishes had to be washed with a particular soap detergent for the grease to completely dissolve before being packed. None of it mattered anymore because it was all in the past.

And today, after all the commotion of packing and moving on out; after all that's been said and done, there is only letting go to do. It sounds simple enough, doesn't it? But I know it is something so many simply cannot do. I am beginning to wonder whether I have the strength to truly move on or fall victim to the trap that is the past.

Standing in the hollow space with great emptiness surrounding me, I take a last look around the place. There are a few large pieces of furniture like the dining table and work desk still to be uprooted. But for now, they are like me and refuse to say good-bye. I leave and take the elevator down to the basement where residents park their vehicles and see a car that is no longer mine. Its new driver is coming later this week to claim ownership and I suddenly wish that I hadn't sold it. He used to joke that this car was his office and at times, a second home to him.

With a heavy heart, I open its door for the last time and sit in the driver's seat. I am still expecting him to come up from behind and ask where I want to go; but logic tells me he won't be doing that. As though on auto-pilot, I reach over and slide open the compartment on the passenger side, to find a notebook. It is brown in color and bounded with soft leather. Perhaps it was meant to be found and as I open the cover, I cannot help but feel crushed yet again to see writing that is all too familiar. As I turn the first page and lay eyes on the words he wrote, I feel as though I am getting to know him all over again:

Some believe life is a gift while others are convinced it is a curse. Many think it hides a great secret reserved only for the strong and mighty and if this secret is discovered, it will offer the greatest luxuries and comforts life could ever give. The ones strong enough to uncover this treasure will in fact find happiness.

But life is not to be worshipped or feared. It is not a test to salvation any more than it is a precursor to hell. It is simply just a journey that the living takes. We all choose to take a certain path hoping that if we walk long enough, this road will give us something good that will make us happy.

Many spend a whole lifetime blindly searching for happiness. They are willing to do just about anything; not caring who they injure or destroy along the way. While they appear righteous and indestructible, these are often the very same people who hide and disguise their vulnerability from those around them. Drugged by their own pride, they refuse to admit that the wrong path was taken and would rather go on wasting their days searching aimlessly than to stop and cherish the very life they were given.

There are those who become tired from searching but grow restless being dormant. While too weary to continue on, they are also too proud and stubborn to admit failure. They waste their days dreaming of taking action, but retreat in hesitation instead. Trapped with indecision, they turn bitter and life withers away as if it never existed for them.

Between these extremes, there will emerge the strong who continue on their journey, overcoming all. Instead of searching for bliss, these people create their happiness. Although fully aware failure is possible, they refuse to succumb and embrace whatever life offers as they brave through their chosen path. While they don't know exactly what the future holds, they do know that as long as they hold true, happiness will find them.

ISAAC

Lesson 1: Average Beginnings Are Not Absolute

My father was a bus driver and my mother was a seamstress. They were your typical couple from a small rural village in China who used a trusted family matchmaker to meet each other. Their union was forged based on logic and practicality. He was a working class man and she also came from a family of average working folk. Neither outweighed each other in education or social status making them a compatible fit in the eyes of their society. Having a child was not a choice, but an expectation to follow the norm; and the decision to move to the big city was fueled by my father's survival instinct. He knew that if we did not move in time to escape the slums of a degrading farmland, the remainder of our days would have left us rotting in poverty.

Apart from the one decision that moved us half way across the world, my parents led average lives that were neither exciting nor glamorous. I saw them coast through life passionless and without meaning. I suppose it wasn't their fault. They were born simple and so were only conditioned to do things for their survival, but nothing more. Naturally, their child who would eventually be their one and only son would also be plain, without having any great success. But that was the wrong assumption.

I suppose I had a fairly normal childhood. My parents always made sure I had enough to eat and clean clothes to wear. I had friends who came and went throughout my life, but I never had a best friend. Once a new school year started, new friends were made and the old abandoned. I was always that old forgotten buddy. I learned quickly that friends were people who used each other to do favours or to pass time when bored- but nothing more. As I grew older, this fact continued to hold true and I gave up making friends altogether. There was no point to friendship and I was fine on my own.

Growing up, my parents never expected much from me, and I sailed through elementary and middle school rather easily. While never excelling in anything, I did pass my subjects that were eventually good enough for college and specialized in Business. I remember choosing Business School because it looked like one of the easier specialties to enroll in and I hated the Sciences. Once there, I had to admit there were instances when I felt the pressure of exams and assignments. But I learned to survive those days using some unorthodox method to ensure a passing mark. A cheat sheet or sweet- talking a teaching assistant for some answers was usually all it took. It didn't happen often, but when those moments occurred, I convinced myself it was a necessary tactic. I did what was needed to be done and so long as it was done selectively and strategically without being detected, it would be as though I had earned the grade honestly.

Despite the absence of great ambition, I did manage to graduate. I remember my parents going through the motions of giving hugs and big smiles as pictures were taken. That day was the only time I ever saw a hint of pride in their eyes. And I remember thinking that perhaps my parents were not always holders of low expectations. Perhaps they secretly did have aspirations for me- their only child, but were afraid that I would fail if they pushed me to try.

"The higher you aim, the greater you fall," was what my father always preached. I think he made himself believe this to help relieve his guilt for not accomplishing anything great in his lifetime. But perhaps seeing me graduate in my cap and gown had given them a kind of relief to know I had finally succeeded in achieving something they never could do.

As school came to an end, I was still the same kid without a purpose or drive. The morning after college graduation, something erupted and I suddenly felt an emptiness I never knew existed. Lying in bed, I began to wonder how life got to be so pointless and decided to blame my parents. I resented them for never teaching me ambition and for never showing me the value of a dream. I faulted them for always feeding me so well that I never felt hungry. It was without knowing hunger that had turned me plain. I began to loathe the average person I had become and the desire to be more grew larger and larger until I couldn't sleep at night.

But time moved on anyways, and my meaningless life took an unexpected turn and made me something more than just average virtually overnight. In a blur, I took my first job in a world of commercial real estate and through some work, alcohol and luck, managed to begin buying buildings that eventually showed me the beauty of money and power. I became addicted to my new found hunger and pushed harder to satisfy the desire to want more of everything. I soon attracted the attention of the media and landed myself on the front of magazine covers. With my face plastered on those pages, it was as though I had finally broke free from my cocoon and people began to notice me. They grew curious of this young man decorated in success and asked about his past- the beginnings of his very existence.

'No', my father was not a Harvard graduate and 'No', my mother was not the daughter of a Chinese ambassador who married my father for some unsaid political gain. Indeed, I was still the son of a bus driver and a seamstress born into an average family that had neither money nor power. I never hid from my past, and found it amusing to see how people reacted whenever I told them about my simple childhood. Some would give pity and then congratulate me for climbing out of an ordinary life, while others simply decided for themselves that I was being too modest and chose not to believe me.

      I didn't care whether they believed me or not. In fact, I didn't care how people regarded me at all. I wasn't naïve and knew that the company I surrounded myself with was only there because of the glamour I had fabricated for myself. In their eyes, I was their American dream and represented wealth and fortune. As long as I stayed rich, they would never leave me alone. As superficial and cold as it was, that was the world I had crafted willingly with my own bare hands. From the moment I uncovered my hunger in the early days, there was no escape or turning back. I knew nothing of happiness or of being content; but only knew of my addiction to triumph over all odds.

      I think it was with this sweet success early in life that led both my parents to their final place of rest together. While they achieved nothing great in their lives, their only son turned out to be someone who was competent and capable enough to fulfill the dreams they themselves could only aspire to in sleep. Perhaps seeing me succeed gave them what they needed to finish a life they never had a passion for in the first place. But whatever it was, their lives ended all the same with a snore and a sigh as they left me to the mercy of this world together in good, but naïve faith. It had been since then that I anticipated life alone, balancing on top of a pinnacle showing nothing but confidence and a refusal to fail. I was determined to never fall victim to average again.

Lesson 2: Accept Unusual Opportunities

It began when Aunt May invited me to lunch. She was mom's best friend and I remember a childhood being filled with frequent visits from her along with gifts and candy treats she would bring for an anxious little boy. I knew that if my own mom had passed away when I was little, she would have taken her place to care for me in an instant. With Aunt May having no children or marriage ties; and me without my parents, we had become each other's family.

I was told that the bond between these two women began long ago when both of them were no more than toddlers living in the same poverty stricken village in China. I envied their connection, amazed of how such two people could maintain a friendship for so long. When one passed, the other continued on as though to keep the bond from also dying.

And so, it was on a Sunday afternoon when she asked me for a favour that would change everything.

"Ai, Ah-Hon," she began in her broken Chinglish- a unique language that intertwined both English and Chinese. Staying true to her Asian heritage, Aunt May would sometimes use my Chinese name, though I preferred to be called 'Isaac'.

"You working too hard these years. Your mother maybe so mad at me now and say I don't take good care of you. I won't have face to see her when it's my turn to go up," Aunt May said, dramatically pointing a finger up above her.

Smiling, I took another sip of my drink as I prepared for another 'life is short' lessons. I had already heard them about a million times but it never ceased to amaze me of Aunt May's continued enthusiasm and energy towards life. Of all the gloom and gray I faced everyday of feign smiles and endless stresses of corporate strategies, she was my one true life source. Oddly enough, Aunt May was my definition of youth. No matter how impatient I was, there was always time to listen to her words of devised wisdom.

"Hon," she repeated. "You work too hard. Even coolies in village in China don't work as hard as you. Life is too short you know."

I nodded as I replied, "I know," half-heartedly. I had heard it all before.

But today was not a day of regular lectures. Aunt May had come with a mission and was determined to get what she wanted.

"I read another magazine today," she began. "Every magazine I see say the same thing. Do you know what they all say?"

Not even the least bit curious, I smiled and answered, "Aunt May, you know I don't pay attention to them. It's a waste of time. I can think of a million other things to do other than read about useless gossip. Most of it probably isn't true anyways."

Shaking her head, Aunt May replied, "Ai-yo...if all magazines say same thing, then it is not all lie."

Chuckling, I gave in and finally asked what Aunt May wanted to hear. "So, what did this magazine say about me then?"

"Magazine say you are like genius in commercial real estate. They say every building you touch turn to gold. They also say you like a machine- only work...so must have sad life because you have only lots of enemies, but no friends or family..."

At that, I raised my eyebrows and with a cold shake of my head chuckled bitterly, "Those bastards. What do they know? I have family- you're sitting right here!" I exclaimed, in-between anger and amusement.

Sighing, Aunt May continued, "Ai-ya...Isaac know what reporter mean. Isaac over 30 now and already very rich, but still don't do anything except work, work, work. Aunt May don't know why you have condo. Isaac can just live in office. If Aunt May not here, I think Isaac never go home for sleep..."

Once again, I could hear the frustration rising in her voice. I didn't want to spend the afternoon arguing over something I knew I would never change. While there may have been some truth to what Aunt May said, I didn't have a choice.

In the world of real estate and investment, clients had great expectations and the stakes were too high. Without anyone to go home to, work was my asylum and was about the only thing that was secure. Work was predictable. I knew as long as I used my head and put my full heart into each project to fight long enough, victory would eventually be mine, one way or another- guaranteed.

People were a different breed altogether. Sometimes seemingly warm and other times devious, there was always something hiding behind a handshake or smile. Humans were calculating and cunning and would not hesitate for a second to destroy a man if it meant for them gaining the upper hand. It had always been that way and I had yet to be proven wrong.

"Aunt May," I finally interrupted. "Can we change topics now? We've gone through this so many times. You know that my work takes a lot out of me."

Sighing and shaking her head in disappointment, Aunt May replied, "So stubborn. Aunt May don't want to bring up, but it's for Isaac's good. That's why you need to do something else- not just work. Aunt May's time is coming soon too and can't look after you forever…"

"Aunt May please..," I interrupted again refusing to listen. But however persistent I was, she was even the more determined to bring her message home.

Holding up her hand she continued on," I have friend, close to your mother too. But when we leave village, we lose contact. Don't see her for so many years until couple months ago at party. She look very old and sick already then."

Shaking her head in sad remembrance Aunt May continued, "Last week, I get call. She die from sickness."

I reached across the table and comforted her with a pat of a hand.

"I'm sorry to hear that Aunt May, really I am. But that's no reason to think your time is next."

Snapping back to her feisty self again, she exclaimed in shock, "Choy, Choy, Choy! Of course I know I'm not going to see your mother yet. Ai-yah! Never pay attention. Isaac so impatient and don't listen- make Aunt May so mad sometime!"

Giving up, I decided not to argue with her anymore, and leaned back in my chair to let my witty mentor talk. I had the time.

"My friend have son, but he also die from same kind of sickness. His wife very bad woman and leave after baby girl born long time ago. So now grand-daughter is the only one left...ai-ya...it is so sad..."

"Did you want me to find a place for her to live? Does she work? I can call a couple of contacts to see if whether there are any positions open. A few of them owe me some favours anyways."

"No, no, no," Aunt May replied shaking her head, "She only a girl how can she work? Only 16."

I nodded my head. Knowing there was more to come.

"Before friend die, I promise her I take care of granddaughter. Your mother would do same thing if still here."

"That's a very noble thing to do Aunt May. If you need any help you know you can ask me."

It seemed that I had finally struck the right chord as Aunt May grinned from ear to ear. At the same time, it dawned on me that there was something more to today's luncheon and it was about to come my way.

"When Aunt May say 'yes' to take care of granddaughter, Aunt May forget she have to go on cruise. That means no one here to take care of her. Aunt May want girl to live with Isaac until I come back from holiday...okay?"

Without a second thought, I shook my head and firmly answered, "No".

Everyday, my life was filled with constant invasions of intrusive speculations and nosy reporters. My home was the only sanctuary where I could experience a little freedom, away from expectations and cruel criticisms. I was not about to let a stranger trample over my refuge and destroy what little privacy I had left in my world.

But Aunt May was never one to give up easily.

"Ai, Ah-Hon," she insisted, "You do so many things all the time everyday. You don't see girl very much. Just tell driver to drive her to school and tell housekeeper to cook and clean room for extra person- that's all."

While I was on my own, to say I lived all by myself in the penthouse would not be entirely true; there was in fact a couple who also stayed with me. I met Mr. and Mrs. Li through Aunt May whom she had first met through a community league of Mah Jong players. Mah Jong or 'MJ' as it was often referred to was a popular Asian game that challenged players of their memory and strategic thinking. It had already saved millions of Asians from boredom in their retirement years.

The Li's had made the big city their home almost half a century ago. Without any children and only each other to call as family, they found themselves retired, but dying of boredom. Over the years Aunt May had hired herself as my housekeeper seeing the mess that would never go away in my home. But she eventually got tired of the job and when she heard Mrs. Li wanted to find work for both her and her husband, she jumped at the opportunity on my behalf.

They turned out to be the best gifts Aunt May had ever given me. No sooner did they move in, my house turned spotless and cleaned to perfection. Virtually over night my clothes were magically cleaned, ironed and hung neatly in my closet while hearty meals appeared on the table every night. Mr. Li- or Henry- as he preferred to be called became my ad-hoc chauffeur, full-time butler and voluntary handyman. And while they were my house aides who collected a monthly salary, they had also become my roommates. While cooking and cleaning for me, they also ate with me at the dinner table and lounged on the couch watching television after a full day's worth of work. I didn't mind them at all. In a way, they were proof that some life still existed at home and between the two of them, my everyday needs were finally taken care of. This meant Aunt May was finally freed from cleaning duties so that she could concentrate on being my full time substitute mother instead.

And though it was Aunt May who brought me Henry and Mrs. Li, to suggest now that I also share them with a complete stranger under my roof was entirely ridiculous. I simply would not have it.

"Aunt May," I replied, "Have you even seen this girl yet?"

Silence. A silence I interpreted as a no.

"You don't know what kind of a person she is- and 16 at that! That's an age where everything is out of control. You always pay attention to my news, but have you taken a look at all the crime happening these days? It's all these crazy teenagers causing chaos."

"Ai-yo! These are bad kids with bad parents. This girl raise by my friend. Must be good one! Only for a couple months…then she live with Aunt May again. Pretend this is charity. Good thing will happen to people who do good thing."

But this time, I would not succumb.

"…No, Aunt May. My mind is already set. I am in no position nor do I have the time to raise a teenager."

"Ai-yo, it's not raising. Aunty May will come back. Think it like babysitting."

"But Aunt May, babysitters get paid. What will I get from this but a rebellious teenager who'll think the whole world owes her?"

In retaliation, Aunt May stared directly at me and fired back, "It will be like repay back all the people you let homeless and jobless every time you buy building or business. It will make Ah-Hon less guilty for all the time you fire good hearted worker."

"Aunt May, that's unfair. That's what I have to do…it's my job!" I exclaimed, defending myself.

"Aunt May of course know. You never have choice right? But now Aunt May give you a choice. Well…?"

With the impatient tap of her finger tips on the table, Aunt May had struck a chord. In fact she had pulled and tugged on my conscience since I got into this business. Her accusations of my seemingly heartless deeds were true but I had always managed to bury them beneath my own ocean of hard emotion glazed without mercy. In a dog eat dog world, I refused to be the eaten at all costs in the name of survival.

But it was getting to be an exhausting day and my mind could not take fatigue's abuse any longer. With Aunt May still determined for an answer of her liking, I quickly searched for the best response that would satisfy both of us for now.

With an exasperated sigh I answered, "I need some time Aunt May. Give me time to think this through. Besides, you don't leave right away."

Figuring that was probably the best she could get from me today, our lunch ended with Aunt May reminding me to call her the minute I reached a decision. And as I hailed a cab and saw her off, Aunt May's endearing ring of continuous squabble pounded my head refusing to leave.

*

A few nights later, I sat in my study and for the first time took notice of the silence that lived with me. During interviews reporters often asked if I was ever lonely living by myself- a bachelor. Never giving any thought, I always answered that work was my life partner. But behind the quick and witty responses, I didn't know what loneliness meant nor what companionship felt like. Besides the periodic excitement that sprang from my work, life for me had always been static with little dynamic spurts. For the first time in my silent fortress I became unsure and was lost. If that was the entrance to loneliness, then perhaps Aunt May was right. I needed to do something else. I needed a voice to clear the stale air that had muffled and suffocated me from life.

  With a sigh, I reached for the phone and dialed Aunt May's number. I wasn't searching for anything in particular; nor was I hoping for any kind of salvation. Simply, I needed to know that I was not the only man living in this world and that there were others. I was just longing for company to provide some comfort; and if company came in the form of a teenager whom I had never met before, then so be it.

*

  The day the girl landed on my doorstep, I didn't even get a chance to speak to Aunt May. She had been so ecstatic to know I had once again yielded to her wishes that she insisted the girl come to my place right away and wouldn't rest until I promised her Henry would pick up the child the very next morning. Little did I realize when I opened my door to find the girl the next day, Aunt May had already left for vacation leaving me to fend for myself.

As Henry dropped the girl off, I caught his eye as he silently mouthed, "Good luck", before leaving me to the mercy of the stranger in front of me.

The teenager was chaos itself, made up of chewing gum meshed between teeth and hair tangled in every direction in a salad bowl of orange and brown dye. Seeing her sent me silently cursing my moment of weakness a hundred times over. She met me with a glare so poisonous I felt venom contaminate my every limb. Without a word, she stayed planted in the doorway as she took her time scrutinizing the man in front of her from head to toe. After what seemed like an eternity, she finally decided to let herself in, swung her bags onto my couch and plopped herself angrily next to it. With the same disgusted look, she began dissecting the rest of her surroundings.

I really did make a mistake. I was desperate for Aunt May to take her back to wherever she had come from. But on the outside, like any trained corporate professional, I remained calm and civil though my insides were squirming with torturous agony.

I called for Mrs. Li to carry her bags to her room. But as my housekeeper stepped towards the girl, both bag and child snapped into one with a threatening hiss of, 'Leave it alone. I'll take care of it myself."

Startled, Mrs. Li glanced back at me as I stepped forward giving her a reassuring pat before she returned to the kitchen to finish the remaining chores that needed to be done. Now in a room by ourselves, I began cautiously, "Umm…I don't know how much Aunt May has told you about me. But this will be your place for the time being. I'm Isaac by the way." Silence…and then more silence.

I tried once more.

"If there's anything you need, let Mrs. Li know. If there's anywhere you need to go, ask Henry. He's the guy who picked you up earlier and is Mrs. Li's husband." Still silence.

As impatience took over, I tried for the last time. "You know, Henry and Mrs. Li is gonna have a hell of a hard time dealing with a mute."

With that, the girl finally shot back, "I only answer to questions worth answering to."

"Well then, what if I asked for your name? Is that worth answering?" I retorted back as anger seeped inside me. I was disgusted with her insolence and once again cursed myself for surrendering to Aunt May's demands.

The child without casting a glance in my direction answered, "Mika. So now can you show me my room?"

Giving up all efforts to being a good host, I showed Mika her room and left without a word.

The rest of the day went on as though the girl had never showed up. Mrs. Li and Henry went about their daily routine as I drove to the office to once again bury myself in paperwork.

As it was the weekend, the office was deserted, but I didn't mind the silence at all. As I plowed through the mountain of files lying lifeless on my desk, I couldn't help but wish for time to slow down just a bit more. The thought of going back to face my new house guest made my stomach churn. How I wished for Aunt May to hurry back home.

Lesson 3: Take Up Responsibility

The first day with Mika passed without much commotion, leaving the very next morning to begin with an exploded panic of Mrs. Li bursting into my room looking for a lost child.

"Isaac! Isaac! Ai ya…. The girl is gone! Someone kidnap her!"

Barely awake from a night of monitoring stock market turmoil, Mrs. Li's squeals reminded me of the nightmare I had brought onto myself. Snapping back to full consciousness, I leaped out of bed and into my robe registering what was just reported.

"What do you mean kidnapped?" I asked, hoping my voice would calm her so that she could tell me the whole story.

In her broken English, Mrs. Li panted, "I go call girl for breakfast this morning and knock on door. But nobody answer when I knock, so me and Henry open the door to check and girl is gone!"

"Are her things still in the room?" I asked, still trying to collect all facts.

Mrs. Li replied, "I think so…don't know. Ai-yo! I should have check on her every hour at night time just in case."

Stepping out into the hallway and shuffling quickly towards Mika's room to check for any belongings, I said to

Mrs. Li, "Don't be silly…the girl's already 16. She should be responsible for her own actions."

Peering in, I saw her bags still lying carelessly in the center of the floor. That at least meant she was planning to come back and reclaim her things, even if she had wanted to stow away.

Turning back to a still shaken Mrs. Li, I offered a smile and patted her shoulder with comforting reassurance.

"Her bags are still here, she'll be back."

Just at that moment, the doorbell rang making both of us jump. Mrs. Li broke into a sprint towards the door only to find the girl waiting impatiently. She appeared much cleaner than the night before, sporting sweats, a tank top and hair tied back. But despite the improvement in attire, she seemed even more fierce and dangerous than the previous day.

Stepping forward I demanded, "Just where have you been? You scared Mrs. Li half to death."

Not at all startled, the girl entered the living room and replied with annoyance, "Geez...what's the big deal? I was out jogging. I run every morning."

"Well you should have told us ahead of time instead of running off like that. We didn't know where you were."

She said nothing while I silently congratulated myself for winning the confrontation. As I turned to leave the room, the girl angrily muttered, "If I knew I was gonna be under house arrest, I wouldn't have come here."

Snapping back to meet her insolent glare, my mind froze with anger so fierce, it blocked all ability to think or speak.

And as I still struggled to find the right fighting words, another demand emerged.

"By the way, I need a key to this place. Don't want to always wake you people up."

With that, she shot up from the couch and dismissed herself leaving Mrs. Li and I staring at each other in disbelief.

*

The week came and went as Mika and I stayed out of each other's way. I gave into her demand of supplying house keys, essentially giving her the freedom to come and go whenever she pleased. I had to admit that the girl was quite resourceful and had an itinerary filled with friends who provided her with entertainment and a mode of transportation as Henry reported the child never once asked for a ride.

By the end of the week, Mika's room looked untouched with her bags still sitting in its original place. I was beginning to suspect that the girl probably never came back home to sleep except for the first night here. And to that revelation, I didn't mind. As long as my work was not disrupted, she could do whatever she pleased. Mrs. Li on the other hand felt differently.

"Isaac, Mrs. Li may be wrong, but this is how I think…"

Hearing Mrs. Li's request for conversation this one morning made me stop working, though I was planning to end the discussion shortly to go back to my file. It was going to be another day filled with meetings and conference calls with no time for me to spare.

"Isaac, I am worry about Mika. I don't think she even come home these days. Bed sheets still clean."

I nodded, still patiently waiting for her to get to the point.

"It look like you know. Why Isaac don't do anything?" asked Mrs. Li, in awe of my indifference.

Growing impatient and not needing to hear any more parenting advice, I asked, "What do you want me to do? I'm not her father."

"Ai-ya…Your Aunty May won't like this. This is very not responsible of you when you say you will take care of Mika."

"Mrs. Li…," I protested, "My responsibility and promise to Aunt May was to provide a roof over her head temporarily. I've already done that and will keep doing that until Aunt May comes back. I promised nothing about being her parent. I don't even have enough time doing my own work let alone play dad to some spoiled brat."

Taken aback, Mrs. Li lowered her head nodding in defeat. Our conversation ended with her picking up the plate that once held my breakfast and had since lost its taste.

Dusting the last remnants of food off me, I grabbed my belongings and headed towards the door. Feeling guilty for snapping at my trusty housekeeper a moment ago, I stopped in my tracks and turned with a soft sigh. "Mrs. Li, can you ask Henry to pick her up from school today? I'll try to come home early tonight and lay out some ground rules for her."

With her face instantly lighting up, Mrs. Li leaped up with satisfaction and clapped her hands as she nodded vigorously chirping, "I prepare extra special food tonight and don't let her go here until Isaac come back."

I nodded and stepped out the door relieved to know that I had left Mrs. Li in better spirits. As I got in the car and headed towards the infinite heights that was downtown, my relief turned to pressure and angst as it did every morning. It was time for work.

*

After an insane day dealing with countless obstacles with project after project, I drove myself home feeling torn and worn down from the chaos I had just endured. It wasn't until sitting at the dinner table and seeing a pouty, angry teenager did I remember the promise I made to Mrs. Li earlier this morning.

With an exasperated sigh, I focused on the girl across the room preparing for another battle. Sensing the tension, Mrs. Li quickly busied herself setting the table and chattering away about her day's activities in hopes of bringing calm to us all.

But I was already feeling patience leave me and knew I would not be able to tolerate any nonsense tonight, especially from a spoiled child.

Henry, always a man of few words, must have saw anger take over the better of me, and feigned a tiny grunt as though clearing his throat. I looked at him as Henry settled in his seat at the dinner table and saw him encourage my patience to stay for just a bit longer. His silent calm seemed to help as I forced myself to take in a deep breath before returning my attention to the girl.

"Mika," I began, determined to take control. "I know you're used to doing anything you want. And I know because of that you're a very independent person. But now that you're living here, I would appreciate it if you followed some guidelines."

With wild eyes, Mika hissed back, "Are you saying that from now on you want me to just sit in my room all day? This is totally unfair! I never got into trouble, what did I do to deserve this…?"

I raised my hands in self defense calming the raving serpent in front of me. "Whoa..." I interrupted. "Slow down there. This isn't punishment. I never said you weren't allowed to go out. For God's sake, don't jump to conclusions. I haven't even told you what I wanted to say."

"Well what exactly are you saying?" challenged Mika, daring me to continue.

"We're concerned about you not coming home these last few nights. I'm not saying you're not allowed to go out with friends; all I'm asking is that I would appreciate it if you at least came back home to sleep so the adults in this house won't have to worry about you. Until Aunt May gets back, I'm responsible for your well-being."

"So, it's all about responsibility again," sneered Mika.

"Well yeah... if you actually know what that word means. Now do I make myself clear of my expectations?"

As though suddenly succumbing to my authority, Mika surrendered and sunk into her chair grunting a weak, "Yes", as she sulked even lower pouting with immature annoyance.

But it didn't matter, because I had just won the battle. Pleased with myself, I returned to the food that was patiently waiting for me. After losing the argument, the girl seemed to have lost her appetite and left the table in an angry huff. We watched Mika make her way to her room, sulking and defeated, as she slammed the door shut against us in one deafening bang.

As the girl's dramatic departure came to an end, both Henry and Mrs. Li quietly looked in my direction. Feeling as though I should say something, I muttered, "I think she got my message."

Perhaps knowing my fatigue, Mrs. Li nodded and replied, "I go and see how she doing." And with that she also left the table and headed towards the girl's room.

Dinner ended that night with Mika's screams piercing through the walls yelling at Mrs. Li for the unreasonable conditions I had placed on her. Walking past her room that had walls too weak to muffle her rage, I wanted to storm in demanding an apology when I felt someone's hand rest firmly on my shoulder.

It was Henry and as I gave him a questioning look, my driver shook his head with a smile saying, "Mrs. Li inside…is ok lah. Girl just need time…she is young." Once again calming my incontrollable temper, I resisted the urge to bolt through the door and instead allowed Mrs. Li to suffer through the girl's abuse. My housekeeper obviously had the patience I didn't have. Giving Henry a reassuring smile, I backed away from the girl's room. As far as I was concerned, my parenting for the day was over.

*

It was a done deal. The bid my company had worked on for so long was finally complete. To the satisfied approval of my superiors and new client, our signatures were sealed on the dotted line of a multi-million dollar project. Victorious days like today always made the job worthwhile.

As the champagne was being uncorked to a newly rejuvenated and inspired team, a phone call came. My assistant Nancy passed the receiver to me, as her expression told me something was wrong.

Clearing my throat, I acknowledged the speaker on the other end saying, "Hello. This is Isaac, is there anything I can do for you?"

What came after was something unexpected and yet at the same time a message that wasn't surprising at all.

"Hello," the voice began. "This is George Malny, the principal of Regionary Secondary college calling. I understand that you are Mika's temporary acting guardian. There seems to be an issue I think we should discuss together as soon as possible."

Hearing the urgency in his voice I agreed to a meeting later that afternoon. Hanging up the phone, I felt Nancy's inquisitive eyes follow me, curious as to what just happened. I turned to her and managed a weak smile telling her I would not return to the office after lunch. Working for me for so many years, Nancy knew it was not the time to ask. And so, without any questions, she left me alone with my silence- company I was all too familiar with.

*

I entered the school's office to find Mika alone slumped in a seat in front of the principal's desk who had yet to arrive. We made eye contact but nothing beyond that. I desperately wished for George Malny to reveal himself soon. The silence between the serpent girl and I was getting to be unbearably toxic.

Finally, the door opened and a man who I assumed arranged today's meeting appeared and introduced himself as George Malny. At first glance, George was an awkward looking man. Short and plump, he moved around with a slight limp and seemed obsessed with adjusting his tie. As I accepted his clammy handshake, I noticed beads of sweat planted loosely on his forehead just above his receding hairline. And before anything more could be said, George Malny blurted, "Oh my goodness! So you *are* that Isaac we see all the time on the news- the one who's the real estate tycoon? Oh wow…I suspected that it may be you, but didn't know for sure…"

Long immune from shallow flattery and looks of wonder from mere strangers, I managed a smile and politely confirmed that I was indeed the Isaac he was talking about. Still in disbelief, the man continued his babbling. "Well it is quite an honour. I absolutely admire you...really I do. I didn't know Mika was associated with such great influences."

From the corner of my eye, I saw Mika roll her eyes repulsed and disgusted at what was just said. For once, I had to agree with her and resisted all temptation from breaking the man's hand that was still tightly clenching mine. Sending a signal of impatience, I broke loose of his slimy grasp and asked whether we could discuss the issue at hand. As though snapping back to reality, George Malny cleared his throat and nodded quickly saying, "Of course!" and the meeting finally began.

Still shaking with the jitters, George turned to open a thick file on his desk. As though wanting to carefully mold his words, he nervously glanced in Mika's direction before turning his attention entirely to me. "I understand that you just became Mika's temporary guardian and so might not be fully informed of Mika's well known reputation at the school."

I nodded, urging him to continue.

"I know you are a busy man, so I'll be straight forward. Mika has been at this school for a year. All her teachers have told me she has so much potential and would excel if she only tried. But so far she has created nothing but trouble. We realize she's going through an exceptionally difficult time at home and we've tried to bend over backwards for her in light of her situation, but she's not making it easy for us or on our students…"

"George," I interrupted impatiently. "Just what exactly has Mika done?"

Glancing at Mika once again, George responded timidly, "In these past months, Mika has been caught cheating on tests, stealing and even harassing her classmates. To these offences, the school has been very discrete and has dealt with internally. However, the violation she has committed this time cannot be left without the attention of her family."

"What exactly did she do this time?" I pressed on, irritated of the long winded speech and annoyed at the girl's continued bitter glare.

"One of our staff members earlier today found her selling these in the bathroom to our students."

The man dropped a small plastic bag of white round pills. This was followed by a silence while anger and embarrassment brewed inside leaving me speechless with rage.

"I know of your contributions to this community and also of your responsibility to Mika. So we wanted to consult with you first before acting on anything. The school is willing to overlook this incident this one time on the condition that we have your personal guarantee something like this will never happen again."

His message was understood while I did nothing but glare at Mika who showed not the slightest remorse or guilt. To her, she had done nothing wrong. The girl was not sorry for her actions and was not even sorry for being caught.

And so, the meeting ended with me expressing my sincerest gratitude for the school's discretion and a personal guarantee that the girl would not do anything of the sort again. Between the handshakes and assurances, there was also a quiet agreement that my contribution to the school's upcoming fundraiser would be substantial enough for them to ignore and dismiss Mika of any wrong doing for awhile.

It didn't surprise me and I wouldn't have expected anything else. Morals and principles were only used to decorate people on the surface, but it never went deeper than that. This was how the world functioned whether it was at school or at work. Once again, it was proven that the world I survived in was nothing more than about money. Favours done rested on the legitimacy of shady verbal contracts and the magnitude of problems simply depended on the weight of secret handshakes and winks involved. Even when dealing with the future of an adolescent drug trafficker, there was no exception because her name was now connected to mine.

The car ride home was driven through a dense fog of silence. With my hands tightly clenching the steering wheel, I felt trickles of sweat being squeezed from the pores of my palms. I was furious, and wanted to wrap my hands around Mika's neck to shake her until she pleaded for mercy. It took every bit of energy I had left in me to convince myself I was much more civilized than to exert physical force on this insolent girl who was slowly becoming more and more my problem. It was a miracle I got us back safe and alive with the anger that fumed inside me the entire time.

When we arrived home, Mika continued to ignore me as I refused to look at her. And that was how the night ended. Henry and Mrs. Li seeing the tension that was beginning to be a familiar scene retired for the day as the girl locked herself in her room again. I knew she was furious of a financial transaction disrupted as I shielded myself in the comforts of my study with Nancy on speaker phone reciting the next day's agenda.

I began to yearn for Aunt May's comforting lectures and found myself missing her life lessons. Then, like a sudden rain cloud, Mika loomed over my mind yet again. Shaking off thoughts of both Aunt May and Mika, I turned my attention to the paper files in front of me once again. I didn't know whether the business I was in did anybody good but at least my transactions were legal.

Lesson 4: Confront Tragedy And Despair

Work at the office the next day was quite peaceful. This was usually expected after closing a big deal. The team needed some time to settle before once again going full force to fulfill the obligations the contract had promised.

With such an uneventful day, I was not prepared for what Henry told me when he drove me home later that night. Peering at me through the rear view mirror, my driver carefully said, "Mika missing again. School phone and say she not there at school today. Do you want to call police?"

Without an inch of a nervous twitch, I shook my head rubbing my temples and answered, "No, she's old enough to know where she lives. She'll come back when she's hungry or out of money."

When we finally returned home, Henry looked at his wife and shook his head before heading out again to run errands. Unrelenting, Mrs. Li took her turn and approached me saying, "Maybe when Mika come back you can talk to her about what happen in school. Mika still young and don't have direction yet. Mr. Isaac should give her time. You know, when she get caught yesterday, she very scared. But she very stubborn and don't admit it."

"She actually told you what happened yesterday?" I asked, surprised of the intimacy I never knew existed between them.

"Ai-ya…It easy with girls," Mrs. Li replied with a twinkle in her eye.

Just as I was about to ask more of their budding friendship, a bang and wail full of alarming despair breached through the front door as if signaling the end of the world was upon us.

The frantic pounding did not stop until Mrs. Li opened the door with me closely at her heels. We found a boy with orange hair and a skeleton earring hanging on his left ear as if warning others he was a dangerous substance. Panting and out of breath, it seemed as though he had lost all certainty, though his eyes housed a similar rage that reminded me of Mika.

Knowing immediately who he was looking for, I passively said, "Mika's not here. You might find her at school tomorrow if she decides to show up."

As I was about to shut the door, his foot blocked my attempt as he pointed upwards still panting, "Mika's on the roof…hurry up before it's too late!"

My heart instantly skipped a beat in fright as I instructed Mrs. Li to call the police while following the boy already miles ahead of me.

Bracing myself to find seriously injured bodies, I was furious to see at first glance a girl and Mika laughing and enjoying the view of the city lights each with a beer in hand. I glared back at the boy who led me to the scene, demanding an explanation. Still trying to catch his breath, he pointed to the ground where only rocks and gravel lay. As I looked closer, I saw that there were other things supporting the beer cans that had been thrown carelessly onto the ground. There were bottles that must have held pills moments ago, but were now empty and I understood.

Fear gripped me tighter yet as the two girls continued their drunken dance and began to balance on the ledge of the building stories upon stories high. They did not care that the edge of the building bridged the border between life and death itself.

I braced myself, careful not to lunge forward too quickly so as to startle the girls, and took a step in their direction. But as intoxicated as she was, Mika was fully alert and slashed her head crazily towards me as the gravel under my feet crackled evilly giving away my intentions.

With a crazy shriek that could have ripped anyone to shreds she slurred ferociously, "D-d-don't come here! Those pills are b-aaaaa-d for you!" In between her mad screams, she continued gulping down the beer and willed the toxin to fuel her with energy and rage. The girl had gone insane and was without fear.

But I refused to relent, knowing I had to gain control of the situation because there was no else that could now. Taking much smaller steps and forbidding my voice to show fear, I calmly reasoned, "How about you and your friend come down from that ledge. It's safer down here and we can talk."

With a disgusted look, she yelled back in a mix of drunken angry slurs, mumbles and growls of, "I won't come down until he comes. No one else in this fuckin world can make me come down!"

Confused, I turned to the boy behind me who was still shaking and terrified. Seeing my puzzled look, he shook his head but offered an answer the best he could mumbling, "I think she's talking about Kyle. He was with her earlier before she started on the beer and pills. I-I-I think they got into a really big fight or something..."

It was understood then that her heart had been broken and slashed to pieces with only drugs and alcohol to console her. But now they were also about to destroy her with one faulty move, possibly dragging her friend with her.

I had to think quickly- anything- to get them off the balcony first, and followed what my instinct told me to do. I lied.

Turning around, I yelled back, "If you're talking about Kyle, he's actually in my living room right now waiting for you."

Hearing this, Mika's motions slowed as she cocked her head to one side as if almost persuaded, but then changed her mind with a drunken claim of, "You're a fuckin lousy liar. You don't even know Kyle!"

"No, I don't know him but he knows you live with me and was looking for you. How else would I know his name? I promise you, I'm not lying. I'll bring you to him. But you have to get off the ledge first!"

Examining me with unstable wild eyes, she confirmed with a slurred speech of, "Y-y-y-ou're not b-b-b-b-sin'g me are you? Cuz-z-z i-f-f-f you are I'm gonna hafta k-k-kill you…"

I nodded feigning scout's honour and braved another step forward barely touching her fingers. Where was help? Mrs. Li should have called the police by now.

Perhaps someone somewhere had enough of the madness and decided to push fate one last time to end it all. But no matter how much analysis is done to find a rationale, and even if an answer was found, nothing will change what happened that ended the night.

Finally deciding that I was telling the truth, Mika reached out to grab my hand while flailing her other arm to claim her balance, beer can still in tow. Maybe it was the rain that turned the gravel into a lumpy slick skating rink, coupled with Mika's drunken state that tipped the beer can out of the girl's grip hitting her friend's face who was still wobbling on the edge of the building. And like a domino effect, her friend lost her balance and tore through the night sky off the edge of the balcony. Her downward surge made a deadly salutation of a sorrowful life before crashing on top of the police car that had just arrived, its sirens wailing to declare to the world that the angel of death had just claimed a life.

*

It's ironic how the weather can play jokes or tease you sometimes. When you're at life's lowest point, the sun can shine so brightly without allowing a single cloud in sight proving that you are in fact, not that important at all. The world will not stop because of you.

This is exactly what happened the following morning when Mother Nature ushered in a new day as if trying to convince us that what happened the night before was all a bad nightmare. But we all knew better.

We learned soon afterwards the life that was lost was called Noel. And when she plunged to her death, I think a part of Mika also died. After the accident, the girl was rushed to the hospital so that her bruises and scratches could be fixed. At the hospital, she did nothing but lay in bed all day with her eyes wide open. And while she was once a wild poisonous snake, the fire that had fueled her existence was lost and could not be found anywhere. All the psychologists, doctors and nurses couldn't break through her wall and she became a piece of lifeless flesh left behind by someone just as empty. I was unprepared to watch Mika slowly self-destruct. For someone who prided himself in bringing back dead buildings to life, I found myself stranded in the distance- useless to this girl who refused to let life in no matter how much I wanted to help.

When she was deemed physically well enough to go home, doctors told me to give her some time.

"It was a traumatic experience after all," they told me. To witness something like that so unexpected could leave someone in shock for awhile.

And so I gave her all the time in the world with her thoughts. To Mrs. Li's dismay, Mika once again became almost invisible to me. Only this time, there were no more squabbles and bickering. It was as if a waking ghost was living with us and I had grown accustomed to it.

Next week, I had a conference to go to and was packing my bags when a quiet and timid knock interrupted my thoughts followed by a Mrs. Li who peered cautiously behind the door. I smiled and invited her to come in.

"When you back?" asked Mrs. Li as she opened the door a little wider.

"In about a week or so."

"Okay…"

I glanced up to see now not only Mrs. Li at the door, but also Henry. They looked like they wanted to say something but wasn't sure how to form their thoughts into the words they needed to say. Seeing this, I stopped everything and sat in the closest chair I could find, waiting until either one of them was ready.

Though mostly the silent one, it was Henry who spoke first. "My cousin who just move to village back home have wife who just call me. He die of heart attack and funeral is next week. I think me and Mrs. Li need to both go back to see him for last time."

Almost overwhelmed of another death plaguing this household, I crossed the room and offered a comforting hug to both replying, "I am so sorry. You take all the time you need. Just give me the invoice after you pay for both your tickets."

With tears of gratitude, Mrs. Li replied, "Thank you Isaac…Mrs. Li don't know what to say…"

Raising my hand and refusing to let her continue, I responded, "It's the least I can do."

While the Li's worked for me, a deeper relationship had since grown between us. Just like Aunt May, they were invaluable and neither of them replaceable. They were a permanent staple in my life and I was beginning to discover they were one of the few people I trusted in this world without a doubt.

Tired of their frowns and worried looks, I wanted to bring back a smile to both their faces, and forced a big grin declaring, "I'm grown up now. I think I know how to cook and drive myself to work."

Returning my smile equally as warm, Mrs. Li replied, "Mrs. Li know, but Mika isn't big girl yet."

Just like that, I was reminded I wasn't alone these days. And as thoughts of a girl curled up in her dark room, dreary and depressed flashed through my mind, Henry continued to speak.

"I drive Mika to visit friend's grave. She cry for so long it almost make me cry too. I think she still blame herself and scare that if she is by herself something bad will happen."

Almost out of desperation, I begged, "Could she not go with the both of you? The countryside could do her some good."

"We do think that, but funeral need to do so many many things…"

And," Mrs. Li chimed in, "no good idea bringing her to another funeral. Ai-ya…too many sad things happen already to her."

Ashamed for suggesting such a thing in the first place, I nodded my head and let out an exasperated sigh, asking, "Then what do you think I should do?"

Knowing he was treading on sensitive waters, Henry answered carefully. "What about Mika go with you? You work anyway, but she have chance to go to different place and have fun."

Not too long ago, I would have refused outright as though it were a natural reflex. But given the circumstances of today, with one life already tragically lost, I couldn't think of another way but to agree with Henry's suggestion.

Seeing the Li's watch me with hopeful eyes, I answered, "I suppose there's a way to book an extra seat on the plane and she can stay in the suite next to mine."

Relieved, and perhaps surprised of my cooperation, the couple excused themselves as they chirped cheerfully down the hall to let Mika know of the exciting news.

I found myself straining my ears through the walls, curious of Mika's reaction; though I didn't know what I wanted to hear. And then, out of thin air, I heard a muffled, "Okay," as Mrs. Li explained to her of the upcoming arrangements.

While I could not detect any emotion in her voice, her acceptance already left me relieved and pleased. Perhaps we were both tired and going away to a different place would be a good thing for us two sad souls.

Lesson 5: How To Mend A Broken Heart

Days later, three people stepped onto a plane together. The journey was peaceful with Mika content on being invisible, withdrawing herself from the world in sleep; while Nancy recited the key highlights of what was to be expected in these next few days of work. We landed with sunlight beaming down on our faces as though welcoming us to a new beginning.

We checked into the hotel and each went into our separate suites to drop off our baggage. By the time we reconvened back in the lobby, there was only about a half hour before my first meeting. We decided that I would go alone to the conference centre for the first part of the day while Nancy graciously volunteered to take Mika out for lunch. I was surprised when she refused to take my credit card.

"It's on me," was her only reply with a twinkle in her eye.

*

Three hours had already passed and the end of the meeting was still far from sight. It was obvious everyone in the room was beginning to suffocate from the air that had turned stale in the midst of squeaking chairs, impatient grunts and clearing of throats hinting that the time was ripe for a break.

In the lobby, I found Mika and Nancy sitting together browsing through a magazine. For the first time in months, I saw Mika smile from something Nancy said. Perhaps there was still hope for the girl.

Glancing up as I approached them, Nancy offered a glowing smile welcoming me to join their all-girl club.

"On break?" asked Nancy as I greeted her question with a nod.

Smiling at Mika, I asked, "So what did you two do all morning?"

Still flipping through the pages of the magazine, Mika answered casually, "Nancy took me out to lunch, and then we went shopping and then sight seeing."

"Sounds like fun."

"Uh-huh," still mesmerized by the images on the pages in front of her.

It wasn't much of a conversation, but somehow it was enough to make my day. Since our first encounter, my interactions with Mika were always filled with yelling matches and bitter glares. It was as though she had labeled me an enemy even before we met. Before today, we never had any exchanges that were calm and subdued.

As though reading my mind, Nancy shot me another smile as though to encourage me on. I threw a large grin back at her in hopes she knew how grateful I was of her kindness.

I checked my watch for the time and said, "Well, I better get back soon. Nancy, you want to come in with me for this last part?"

Hearing this, Mika looked up like a puppy about to be abandoned and asked, "Should I go back to my room?"

Unsure of what to say, I caught Nancy's eye as she silently reminded me to be gentle with my response.

Perhaps it was the summer heat or the surprising change I saw in Mika that led me to suggest she could also join the meeting as an observer.

Once again, it was the three of us- this time entering the conference room. I introduced Mika as an inspiring youth who was job shadowing me and invited her to take a seat in the back of the room. Nancy took her usual place beside me at the table ready to be the exceptional assistant that she was. We all played our roles flawlessly.

The meeting was finally adjourned another three hours later. Rising from my seat, I expected to find Mika slumped over her chair, worn down by boredom. But instead, she was already standing by the door waiting for us, alert as ever.

Bidding the rest of my colleagues a farewell for the night, Nancy and I made our way towards Mika. It had been a long day and all of us were relieved to be released from the shackles of our work.

Upon approaching Mika, I suggested, "Why don't we get something to eat?"

Met with eager nods, I escorted both of them to my car and drove to the restaurant I remembered that served the best red wine and steak.

When we arrived, I requested the table that had a waterfront view facing the mountains that surrounded a city skyline decorated with the brilliance of its bright lights. I hoped the view soothed my companions the same way it did for me. As Nancy and Mika soaked in what lay before them, both gasped in amazement, speechless. I knew then that the magic of the mountains and water Mother Nature created had once again mesmerized her audience. Both were equally hypnotized by the tranquility many of us deprive ourselves from in this crazy world.

"Everything here is so expensive!" exclaimed Mika as we explored the menu.

"It's a good thing that you and I aren't paying then, eh?" teased Nancy who smiled at me mischievously.

I smiled back, equally as playful and responded, "I think I can still afford a meal or two here."

Unconvinced, Mika asked, "Are you sure?"

"Give it your best shot."

Taking up my challenge, Mika looked up and smiled. When the waiter came to take our order, she pointed at the most expensive entrée with the expectation that I would live up to my word. The girl certainly had a zest for competition.

And so the night went on with the three of us enjoying our food and each other's company. For the first time in a long while, there was laughter at the dinner table. For me, I couldn't remember the last time I had laughed at a joke or comment simply because it completely amused me. For the first time in a long time, there was honesty without pretense. Even if it was for only the one night, I was at last released from all constraints and was liberated.

I also knew it was the first time for Mika to have a real meal without any burdens suffocating her appetite. The weight that had crushed her liveliness was forgotten for now; and in its place she had found friendship to keep her warm and content.

*

Later that night, I was startled awake to a banging on the door as though the world was about to end yet again. Still half asleep, I jumped from my bed to open the door and was surprised to see a frazzled Nancy trembling in sheer panic.

"Hurry! Upstairs on the roof!" commanded Nancy already making her way down the hall as quickly as she had come to my door.

I chased after her, still deciding whether I was dreaming or if this was reality.

While running and almost catching up to Nancy I called out, "What's going on?"

Electing to use the stairway, Nancy panted, "It's Mika. Security just called and said there's a teenage girl on the roof going hysterical and threatening to jump. The hotel said they recognize the girl to be with us."

"What?!" I exclaimed in disbelief. Already thoughts raced through my mind not believing what I just heard. Was the night that had just past a few hours ago a figment of my imagination? Surely this was not really happening.

As we reached the rooftop, it was like déjà vu all over again. We found four security guards anxiously guarding the doorway. Seeing us approach, one of them stepped forward and reported, "We thought you might want to settle this low key, so we didn't contact the police yet. We figured that as long as she's far away from the ledge she won't be a hazard to herself."

Dumbfounded of such a senseless decision, both Nancy and I shrieked, "What?!"

"What the hell are you guys thinking? Call 911 immediately unless you're willing to take responsibility if anything happens. Call the police right now damn it!" I commanded as though I was God himself.

Shaken by our reaction, the man mumbled his apologies and called for police assistance to be immediately sent to the hotel.

Meanwhile, Nancy was already slowly advancing towards Mika who was clenching a beer bottle ever so tightly while wailing a storm of tears and desperate cries of anger that I had already heard before not so many nights ago.

Mindful of her words and conscious of the distance between herself and Mika, Nancy asked as calmly as she could, "Mika, what's the matter? What happened?"

In a blurb of drunken whimpers, she replied, "I killed someone. I deserve to die. I really should die!"

"What do you mean you killed someone? Don't be afraid, you can tell me. No one is here to hurt you. We only want to help."

Deranged, but still able to drag her drunken feet below her every which way, the girl slurred, "I k-k-killed Noel! The whole world knows it and I can't pretend nothing happened!"

Though saddened to know she was still torturing herself over her friend's death, I breathed in a sigh of relief to know that the girl didn't literally take someone's life.

Not knowing what to do, Nancy turned to me for help afraid to do anything that could hurt the fragile child in front of us. By now, police officers had arrived, but I motioned for them to halt allowing only Nancy and I to approach Mika.

It was my turn to talk to the girl. I stepped forward and began in earnest saying, "Mika, I was there that night, remember? Noel slipped herself, it was an accident and wasn't anyone's fault."

Shrieking back, she yelled, "Shut up! What do you know? I was the one who got her drunk and high on those pills. I was the one who dragged her on the roof and I was the one who was supposed to fall off the roof, not her! You don't understand!"

Heart frantically pumping, I barked back angrily like a mad dog, "Then fine! Jump now then, what are you waiting for?"

I ignored Nancy's tightening grip on my arm that warned me to stop my madness, and continued to shriek, "If you had the guts, you would have jumped after her that night. Why didn't you?"

As Mika's drunken moans and wails grew louder and more desperate, I broke free from Nancy's grip and moved in closer, pushing myself to continue on.

"You think that by jumping Noel will thank you? Quit being so selfish and grow up. By dying, you'll only make yourself feel better you idiot!"

Through my yelling, I grew fearless and was determined to beat Mika down. I had to get through to her and make her see that she had no right to take anyone's life- including her own.

With cries of self-pity being drowned out by my overpowering screams, the girl suddenly collapsed and reduced herself into a shriveled ball, willing the ground beneath to swallow her whole. The girl had dragged her shaky hands over her ears begging me to stop torturing her with my words.

Nancy took this chance and ran towards Mika, hugging her like a mother would for her child in pain. Knowing the girl was now safe in Nancy's embrace, I turned back to the police and security guards who were all amazed of what just transpired and asked for a doctor.

When first aid finally arrived, we were still on the roof as if frozen in time. Nancy was holding Mika rocking her back and forth, as the girl's cries pierced the night sky, willing Noel to hear them. And through it all, Nancy gave me a reassuring nod, her eyes promising me the end to the fiasco would be over soon and all would be well once again.

I carried the child in my arms after sedatives were administered. Once safely in bed, I returned to the hotel staff giving them specific instructions of what to say to the media that would soon be pestering everyone, and made them aware of the consequences if anyone disobeyed my instructions. I would not allow any more harm come to Mika. She had endured enough.

Finished with my orders and returning to Mika's room, I found Nancy kneeling beside the child's bed side. While she had just gotten to know the girl, it was obvious Nancy had taken a liking to Mika and was troubled over what was just witnessed. Placing a hand on Nancy's shoulders, I whispered, "We should probably let her rest."

Nodding, Nancy got up and followed me out into the living room. As I stepped onto the carpet floor, a crumpled ball of newspaper prickled the bottom of my feet as I instinctively bounced back as though it were poison; afraid that any noise would wake Mika from her slumber. Retrieving the piece of garbage off the floor, Nancy looked at the article and gasped in horror. I followed Nancy's eyes and saw in huge bolded letters a headline reading: *Girl Kills Friend in Love Triangle Squabble.*

Furious, I tore the paper from Nancy's hands and whipped it over the balcony as though it would disintegrate into thin air. Behind me, Nancy offered a comforting pat on my shoulder.

Sighing, she said, "At least you know what happened."

Staring aimlessly, I replied bitterly, "She's just a kid. I don't see how or why they would prey on her with these lies. It's just sick!"

"Not all of it is untrue, Isaac…"

Whipping around so that I was hovering over Nancy like an angry bear, I dared her to continue. I couldn't believe what she was saying. A moment ago she had been Mika's protector and now she was defending those ruthless people that had stripped away a child's dignity, nearly destroying her life.

Protecting herself from my rage, Nancy quickly said, "I'm not defending them. Mika told me today a little bit of what happened. Her friend who died had been involved with a boy who Mika was also dating. So in a way it was a love triangle as they say. But the reporters didn't have a right to depict the accident the way they did. That was wrong."

Sorry for letting my temper run wild so quickly, I let down my guard and released a sigh as I nodded in apology and turned away from Nancy. I stared at the night sky hoping that a falling star would guide my next course of action for I was completely lost. I wasn't supposed to feel this helpless and concerned for this child. The Isaac I knew would have been completely indifferent, dismissing the girl as an immature brat who brought this all onto herself. There were many things in this world that mattered more than puppy love. But somehow, I found myself sympathetic and feeling pity for Mika and was disappointed in myself for failing to support and protect a child I had promised to take care of.

"Could I offer some advice?" peeped Nancy as though apologetic in disrupting my thoughts.

I nodded waiting for her to continue.

"Tomorrow, when we see Mika, let's not ask her any questions and just take care of her physical needs. Give her the benefit of the doubt and let her talk when she's ready on her own terms."

"I can't pretend nothing happened. Damn it, she almost killed herself for the second time!"

"I know, but I also have a feeling that Mika can't be rushed. Trust that she'll come around on her own time. It's the only way to get through to her." Beaten and defeated, I gave in and released all the anger, despair and fatigue this night had brought forth with an exasperated sigh.

"If you're still worried, let me talk to her then. It's easier between girls," offered Nancy, as her smile returned to comfort me.

Grateful for her help, I repeated, "Easier between girls. That's what Mrs. Li says too."

Shooting back an exhausted smile, Nancy said, "I better go. Tomorrow's the weekend so you won't need me for work. Let me take her around town- just the two of us. Don't worry Isaac, she just needs time."

Escorting her to the door, I thanked Nancy for the last time that night and let her out. Turning back, I peered into the room where Mika was still sleeping peacefully, and found comfort knowing she was protected in restful slumber.

I headed back to the living room and plopped myself onto the couch like a dead fish, thinking. Nancy had said time was what Mika needed; but did it have the needed resilience to break down the wall that had imprisoned the girl away from the world for so long?

I was starting to understand that her anger and bitterness was nothing but armour she had made to protect herself from all the hardships she had already endured in this young life of hers. I suppose in a way, it was like the mask I used everyday to barricade myself from those who could trample me, so that I would not be harmed.

But tonight showed just how fragile we all were. Nancy was right. I wasn't the person to preach to Mika because I was just like her. It suddenly dawned on me that if we both continued to be this jaded and bitter, we would eventually drag ourselves further away from reality until we slowly withered down into nothingness. I couldn't let that happen. The fright I faced tonight was too much, too real. Time was what I needed to pull both Mika and I back into something that believed in goodness. And if one of us still had to be left behind in a sad world, I would rather that person be me. At least then, I would have left the world knowing I gave someone back their faith saving them from anymore regret.

*

She stumbled into the dining room the next morning looking hung over and exhausted, but overall intact. We made eye contact but nothing more. Remembering Nancy's advice, I poured hot breakfast into her bowl and offered it to her. She stared at the food, glanced at me and then back at the bowl asking, "Did you make this yourself?"

I nodded answering, "Yeah, too lazy to call room service."

"But you weren't too lazy to actually cook yourself."

Her sharp wit made me feel silly as I smiled with embarrassment. I was still trying to decide whether the girl was alright or was she merely putting on an act to avoid pity. I felt like I was on a sheet of ice not knowing whether it was thick enough to walk on or would it crack and break underneath my weight.

Watching Mika eat her breakfast, I also turned to my food and continued reading my newspaper in silence. Not a word was uttered between the two of us as I allowed Mika eat in peace. It was better to glide along naturally than to force something ahead of its time. As the girl finished her breakfast, I cleared my throat and casually mentioned, "Nancy's off today and she was saying that she needed someone to go shopping with her. You interested?"

Picking at the last morsel of porridge in her bowl and without looking up, she answered, "Yeah, sure."

I jumped from my seat and phoned Nancy to solidify their date. Just as thrilled, Nancy promised to come for Mika in an hour's time.

There was a knock at the door precisely an hour later and I opened it to find Nancy, refreshed and smiling to welcome all of us to a new day. It was a big difference from the woman who had screamed bloody murder the night before.

Happily succumbing to her energy, I invited Nancy in as we waited for Mika. Nothing was mentioned of the bedlam that had ensued last night. It wasn't because it was a taboo subject, but rather, there was no use bringing up the past, no matter how recent, as nothing could be undone. What we could do instead was to silently help each other move forward using the past to merely guide the way we wanted to go.

    Mika finally appeared in the living room and lit up to see that her new friend had already arrived. The girls left shortly afterwards leaving me to stay in silence's company. Yet, this silence wasn't nearly as comforting as the one that was here a moment ago when I was with Nancy. In fact, it was a form of silence that was depressing and simply annoying. Faced with this on my own, I dealt with it as I always did and drowned myself in work as though there was no tomorrow.

MIKA

Lesson 6: To Simply Change Yourself

When Isaac's cooking woke me up this morning, I wasn't totally sure if last night actually did happen. It felt so safe hiding under the sheets; it was like I was in a different world. But that was just wishful thinking. I knew the truth and dragged myself out of bed tired, embarrassed and sad.

But everyone looked like they had forgotten the whole thing and I was happy to do the same. So the day started with me and Nancy shopping for clothes and trying on things we thought we could only wear in our wildest dreams. I gave her advice on what looked good on her; and she told me the truth when something looked horrible on me.

Hanging out with Nancy made me feel like a normal person again. I had never been able to call anywhere home, but my place with Nancy felt right. I would have given up anything to feel the way I did forever.

After shopping, we had lunch and before I could ask Nancy if we could catch a movie, she took my arm and said she felt like a change of scenery. It made me curious, and I gave up on my movie idea and let her drive us to wherever she wanted.

When I asked where we were going, Nancy only said, "You'll see," as if she had a big secret. I knew I wasn't going to get a straight answer, and stared out the window of the moving car instead. It looked like we were driving away from the crazy mess of downtown buildings and into green pasture. It seemed like the more we drove, the more green there was. With so much grass, I couldn't help but feel relaxed and let myself sleep. I didn't really care where we were going anymore because I was already in heaven.

But my nap ended way too quick with Nancy gently shaking me awake. I opened my eyes happy to see that there was still so much green grass around us. Only now, there was also what looked like some kind of temple a few feet away and when we got out of the car, I could smell incense.

I looked at Nancy, completely lost. I had no idea why we were here or what she wanted us to do. But all she did was tell me to walk quicker up the steps to get to the temple. The closer we got to the top, the louder the chanting got. While I didn't understand a word, listening to them hum, somehow made me feel not as messed up. It was a really weird feeling- but in a good way I guess.

We finally made it to the top and I saw that it was actually a bunch of monks all sitting cross-legged with their eyes closed who were singing the weird chants I had heard coming up here. They looked like they were humming to a gigantic statue in the back of the room. Nancy told me this was the temple's great God- their Buddha. In the centre was a huge cauldron with a bunch of incense that were half burnt, but still had a smell strong enough to make my eyes tear up. I stood there probably looking like a lost kid, while Nancy grabbed a handful of incense for the both of us. Instinctively, I took a few sticks from her, kneeled and closed my eyes with the burning incense in my hands. What was I supposed to think about? Maybe this was my chance to wish for something to come true. From the outside, I betcha it looked like I knew what I was doing, but I was really just copying Nancy and everyone else around me. My mind was a complete blank, I had no idea what was going on and didn't feel like asking.

But we weren't done yet. After bowing three times, I followed everyone again and got up to stick the incense inside the cauldron. As we were about to leave, an old lady in a cotton gray gown and black cap came up to us and offered to read our fortune for a small donation. I was curious, but before I was able to take her up on the offer, Nancy had already politely said, "No, thank you."

Instead, she made me follow her and soon we were behind the temple walking on a small beaten pathway that took us to a place that had more green grass and a mini-waterfall. I climbed on top of a nearby boulder and plopped myself down before realizing just how exhausted I was. Between the quiet and relaxing water noises, I heard Nancy sigh and turned to her asking, "Tired?"

She replied with a grin, "Yeah, a little. But this place has a way of making you lazy."

I knew exactly what she meant and said, "No kidding. How did you find this place anyways?" With a pause Nancy answered, "A friend brought me here a long time ago. He said that it could calm anyone down."

"Working with Isaac is that stressful, eh?" I teased.

Chuckling, Nancy replied, "It can be, but I knew about this place way before I even worked for him." Playing with a broken twig, I didn't say anything because I could tell that Nancy wanted to tell me something else.

"When I was a kid, my parents were always fighting. Sometimes it was just yelling and screaming but there were other times when the fights got pretty violent. When I was growing up, I always hated going home after school because I never knew if my parents had already argued earlier that day or whether another fight was about to come later that night. I just got so fed up with all the tension and angry people in the house."

I wanted to know more and asked, "So your friend brought you here to get away from everything?"

Nancy nodded saying, "It was better than drugs and alcohol. Believe it or not, I never tried any of those things except for some drinking but I couldn't stand the hang-over afterwards. I was too chicken to face my problems, so this place was just perfect for me to hide from everything without the side-effects."

Without thinking, I answered, "Yeah I guess...at least nobody gets hurt coming here...or killed."

"Mika, you know what I think?" offered Nancy. "People complicate life by mixing everything up into one huge dramatic mess. Look at your life for example. If you took a step back and looked at the bigger picture, I bet there are probably a lot of things that aren't such a big deal."

What the hell just happened? One minute she was my friend and then from nowhere, it was like she punched me in the face- hard. She didn't have a right to make any kind of judgment on me when she didn't know half of what I've been through.

But before I could defend myself, Nancy was already talking again. "I'm not under-estimating the crap you had to go through before. I haven't known you for very long, but I can bet that what you have gone through has been because of irresponsible people in your life. Bad things happen to good people all the time, and it might make doing the right thing difficult; but that certainly doesn't excuse you from trying altogether."

Fuming, I replied back bitterly and with clenched teeth, "I don't know what the hell you're talking about."

"Well, take the incident with Noel for example. Yes, you were wrong for taking the drugs and for getting each other drunk on the roof. That was a fault you have to own up to and I think you already have. But as for Noel falling off the roof and dying, that was out of everyone's control- even yours. Nobody can stop you if you want to blame yourself, but how is that going to make things better? When a person dies Mika, they're gone- end of story. It's the people who are left behind who are responsible to learn from their mistakes so that the death didn't happen in vain."

"Why should I be responsible when everyone else gets to do whatever the hell they want and make my life a living hell?" I snapped back. If Nancy thought I was just going to sit back and have her take free swings at my life that she knew nothing about- she was wrong...so very very wrong.

"Nobody's perfect Mika. Everyone makes mistakes- some more than others. But there are always choices. Except for our parents, there are almost always choices in life. You can't control how people behave- even if they are your family, but you can control yourself and your actions. A lot of the time, when bad stuff happens, people become scared and end up hiding from their problems rather than dealing with them head on."

"That's bullshit. Didn't you just say you came here to get away from your problems? You're running away too."

"True. This here is a perfect hiding place- but it's not for forever. We need to escape sometimes to calm down, collect our thoughts and decide what they should do before dealing with the problems again. Kinda like a time out."

I knew Nancy was probably watching and waiting for me to challenge her again. I wanted to, but for some reason, I couldn't. Nancy must have known it too, because she started to talk again.

"You're not a bad person Mika. For you to be so sad from your friend's accident already shows that. I just think you've been lost for awhile and have been trying to find your way. But you keep on getting stuck with all the crap that gets thrown at you and it's making you more and more frustrated with life to the point now you're stuck in self-pity. Believe it or not, everyone goes through this phase once in awhile. But some people choose to never get out of this rut probably because they become scared.

"What makes you think I'm feeling sorry for myself? I've never asked anyone for sympathy ….Not when my no good of a tramp mother left me; not when my loser of a dad died…I've never asked for anything!" I protested angrily.

"No, you might never have asked outright, but your actions certainly have said otherwise. Skipping school, getting into the drugs and alcohol and putting out a 'I don't care attitude'- all tell people that you're pissed off. Besides, don't tell me you've never asked yourself why you didn't have good parents, or at least a good home. You might not have ever asked for sympathy but you can't tell me you've never thought about how unfair life has been to you. Mika, I just really hope you won't be one of those people who can't get back on their feet. You deserve a life better than the one you're living now. You owe it to yourself to treat yourself better- especially after all that you've had to deal with already."

What the hell was wrong with me today? Again, no matter how hard I wanted to fight back and show her how little she knew of me and everything else, I couldn't do it. Maybe because deep down inside, I knew that everything she said was true; and when truth gets in your face like a big bully, there's nothing in this world that can help you run away from it.

Even after Nancy's hugs telling me that everything will eventually work itself out; even after leaving the temple and driving back to the real world, there was something really different now. I guess I was different.

For whatever reason, I wasn't mad anymore; and couldn't remember exactly the things that had made me so scared before, that I couldn't even live a normal life. I couldn't explain what Nancy had done. Only that after her talk- after hearing her lay it out in front of me the way it was, it felt like I was given permission to let go of whatever it was that had made me freak out. And while I couldn't say for sure that I was happy just yet, to feel the way I felt now- lighter and free was still awesome.

ISAAC

Lesson 7: Life's Simple Pleasures

It was once again a peaceful trip back home. Mika hibernated during the entire flight while Nancy and I went over next week's schedule. While nothing more was mentioned about the fiasco that had frightened all of us a few nights ago, I couldn't help notice that something was different.

There was a certain kind of serenity that seemed to have transformed Mika ever since her outing with Nancy. When I asked Nancy, she briefly described a day filled with shopping therapy and a short visit to a Buddhist temple out in the country side- but no more details were shared. When I tried to pry further, Nancy simply refused saying, "It's really Mika's story. She should be the one telling you." Mika had certainly made a great friend on this trip.

I decided not to pursue Nancy or Mika of what had transpired that day. Watching Mika rest peacefully and Nancy's comforting smile reassured me that all was well, and that was really all I needed to know.

Once the plane landed, we got our luggage and found Henry at the gate with a big smile welcoming us back onto home soil. We drove Nancy back to her apartment before heading home ourselves. The car ride with only Mika and I was mostly filled with silence except for Henry's report of how their visit to their hometown went and asking whether our trip was enjoyable.

Mrs. Li was at the door excited as ever for our return and announced she was making an abundance of special dishes to celebrate our homecoming. With her hugs and beaming smile, it was as though we had been gone for years rather than just a few days. And while it was amusing to see Mrs. Li fuss all over us, I was comforted to see her and Henry again. It would have been even more joyous if Aunt May was here with us. Since Mika's arrival, Aunt May hadn't contacted me at all and I was beginning to wonder if she was having a good time on her trip, meeting friends and enjoying life as she always did.

But all thoughts were interrupted as I watched Mika head to her room and shut the door quietly behind her. With Mika out of sight, Mrs. Li asked how the girl was and to her satisfaction I replied that all was well.

"See? I tell you it was good idea right? Mrs. Li always have good idea," my trusty housekeeper proudly declared. With Henry chuckling, I couldn't agree more.

Unpacking in my room, I didn't realize just how exhausted I was. Tomorrow was another work day and I promised myself that I would retire early to bed after dinner.

Later that night, Mrs. Li did not disappoint and prepared a big meal for us made with great portions of love and care. I realized that all of the dishes were either favorites of mine or Mika's and was impressed of how Mrs. Li had been able to discover Mika's food preferences despite knowing the girl for only a few short months.

We enjoyed the evening, exchanging stories of what happened on our trips while I did most of the listening. The funeral back in the village went well despite the few squabbles over final arrangements all large families go through. While grateful to have been able to visit their home roots, both Henry and Mrs. Li admitted it was a relief to be back in the city again.

"Away too long. Not get used to big family anymore. Too much talk about this son and that daughter…lots of gossip…make us tired," was Henry's explanation as his wife nodded in agreement.

I could tell Mika was also amused of their rendition of the trip. Once again, I surprised myself to find comfort in Mika's laughter as Mrs. Li recounted how she almost dropped their cremated cousin's urn when it was unexpectedly thrust in her hands because a relative had to attend to their toddler son who really had to go "pee-pee" during the cremation ceremony.

And as the whole table roared in laughter, Mrs. Li gave a pout and lightly punched Henry in the arm exclaiming, "Why you laugh? He your cousin, you should have help me. If I had drop, don't know what would happen."

And as Mrs. Li scolded her husband, it occurred to me we were laughing at the expense of someone's passing. I hoped that we would not anger the spirits of the departed and silently wished that they would also share in our humour.

As if reading my mind, Mika asked in between giggles, "Should we be laughing at someone's funeral? It's kinda disrespectful and bad karma isn't?"

"Huh? What karma -ah?" responded Mrs. Li. "Ai-yo…no worry lah…cousin very open mind. He probably laugh when his spirit see me too."

And with Mrs. Li's reassurance, we all gave a last chuckle, and silently wished their dearly departed cousin well before moving onto the next topic with Henry asking Mika, "What you do last week Mika?"

I held my breath in anticipation, secretly hoping she would share what Nancy and she did during their time alone together. Mika looked in my direction and paused for a moment as though wanting to carefully pick her words before responding.

Casually shrugging her shoulders, she began, "Nothing much. Plane ride was pretty dull, but the hotel was nice. Got a chance to go out with Nancy and do some shopping and stuff while Isaac worked."

Curiosity got the better of me and before I could restrain myself I blurted, "Nancy told me you guys also got to visit a Buddhist temple. How did that go?"

Unwavering, Mika replied, "It was really nice. I've never gone to one of those before. But it was really peaceful and quiet. Kinda nice to go to those kind of places to get away, you know?"

And with a smile, she added, "Someone even offered to read our fortune when we were there. I wanted to, but Nancy said 'no' so we didn't. It's too bad though. I want to find out whether I'll be a millionaire or not one of these days."

"Ai-ya," scolded Mrs. Li once again. "You so young…no need to believe those things. Lots of people are fake and lie to young girls like you."

Nodding, Mika responded, "Probably. But it would still be nice to know…just for fun."

As the chatter continued, I leaned back in my chair drinking in the moment. Mika's recount of her trip with Nancy, though short as it was, gave me what I wanted to know most- that whatever happened at the temple, gave the strength the girl needed to get up from her fall and move on. To my surprise, it was with this sudden revelation did I find a sense of self-content

I never knew possible for me until now. Was this happiness in disguise?

Lesson 8: Closure

Dinner ended too quickly with all of us retiring to sleep, pleasantly exhausted early in the night. Still relishing in my new found happiness, I was beginning to doze off when I heard a soft knock and found Mrs. Li behind my door.

We apparently had a visitor who wanted to see Mika. Clever Mrs. Li decided it would be best to let me talk to our guest first before bringing him to the girl. Annoyed that the person would pick such an hour to make a house call, yet curious at the same time, I grabbed my robe and headed towards the living room where Mrs. Li had placed him.

I saw someone who was clean shaven, dressed in simple jeans and a T-shirt. He didn't know that someone else was in the room with him and was still lost in his own thoughts. As I cleared my throat, the boy seemed startled by the sudden breach of silence and whisked around to face me.

I noticed his hair was stained a faded brown and the face looked vaguely familiar. I remembered then, that he was the one who had stormed into my home some nights before in sheer terror leading me to Mika's feat on the roof. But tonight, while he still looked the same on the outside, everything else about him was a little different. He was more tame, his anger under control, though there was still a look of fear about him as he shuffled his feet, a little shy and uneasy.

Surprised to see me and not his friend, the boy asked, "Is Mika not here?"

"She is, but she's just got off the plane from a trip and really tired. Maybe you can come back tomorrow night?" I suggested, while inviting the boy to take a seat.

As he found himself a place on the couch, a look of relief took over as he replied, "I don't know if I can tomorrow but just as long as she's alright."

Puzzled, I asked, "Why wouldn't she be alright?"

"I tried calling her, but she didn't answer her phone for the whole week. I tried asking her friends, but all of them haven't seen her for a long time and just the other day, I saw some newspaper headline…"

Settling his worries, I briefly explained to him where Mika had been this past week, without recounting the second rooftop fiasco that had happened to spare the boy from any more sleepless nights.

With nothing else left to say, the boy got up signaling the end of his visit. I promised him I would let Mika know that he had come, but he insisted it wasn't necessary. As long as everything was alright with her there was no need.

As we approached the doorway, I found myself offering a ride home to the boy so that he didn't have to take the bus. Surprised of the offer, he politely declined, but I insisted and we soon found us in my car driving him home.

"I'm sorry, but I never got your name," I asked once we were in the car, trying to break the awkward silence.

"Oh sorry…It's Steve."

Falling quiet once again, I continued with more questions. I found out he lived with his parents and was the oldest out of three boys. He knew Mika through school ever since they were in Kindergarten. Essentially, they were childhood friends.

But now, it was Steve's turn to ask questions, though his concerns were not about me, but of Mika.

"Is she feeling better now?"

Using the same smile I always used to comfort Mrs. Li, I reassured him the girl was going to be fine. Physically, she had recuperated from the night while emotionally, she wasn't completely healed; though I was confident that with rest and some more time, Mika would pull through fully and be whole once more. I believed she was already on the mend.

"You seem to really care about Mika, Steve. She's lucky to have a friend like you."

Blushing, where even the darkness could not hide his flushed cheeks, he looked down mumbling, "Naw…I've known her for a long time. She's a really cool person and I don't want anything to happen to her- that's all."

Silently comforted that Mika had a friend, the rest of the drive was done in silence as we resigned to each of our own thoughts.

Finally arriving at our destination, I pulled up onto the driveway, and as Steve got out of the car, I thanked him on behalf of Mika and invited him to come by for a visit again anytime. Grateful for the ride home and open invitation, the boy thanked me a last time and shut the car door behind him.

Lesson 9: Find Respect

After a full day's worth of work the next day, I came home to a surprise. With Mrs. Li out running errands, I found Mika on the rooftop yet again. But this time, she was in the garden with Henry watering the plants and flowers. With all the chaos that had ensued in these last few weeks the plants had become discolored and the flowers were beginning to wilt. It was as though they were punishing us for neglecting them all this time by destroying their beauty with their own free will.

As I approached them, Henry greeted me with a smile while Mika gave a quick nod before returning her attention back to the nature that lay in front. Passing the hose over to the girl, Henry dusted off his hands and announced, "I go now."

Surprised and taken aback, I asked, "I'm sorry, did I interrupt something? Henry, you don't have to leave."

Patting my shoulder, Henry replied, "No lah…Henry only help Miss. Mika, but you can be her helper now. Henry have to wash car before Mrs. Li come back." Turning back to Mika he said, "You make sure flowers have enough water okay? Flowers still very young but lots of water can still save them." Promising Henry with a nod, Mika continued her duty of tending to the flowers, focused and determined to nurture them fully back to life.

Giving one final pat on my back and still sporting his contagious smile, Henry headed for the door leaving me alone with the girl.

With Henry gone I shuffled closer to where Mika was, unsure of what to do next. Still spraying water on the plants the girl asked, "Why do you even have flowers when you don't take care of them?"

Flustered, I sputtered back defensively, "When I first moved in, it was pretty empty up here. Mrs. Li suggested having a garden and I figured why not."

Met with silence of a girl in thought, I grew curious and said, "Why you ask?"

With a furrowed brow, she cocked her head to one side as though frustrated and said, "Just don't understand why you would make the effort and then leave it just like that. It's sort of irresponsible, isn't?"

Taken aback, I protested saying that Mrs. Li normally took care of the plants.

Shaking her head in disapproval as she carefully picked the dead leaves off my flowers, she replied, "Mrs. Li isn't superwoman you know. She can't do everything and you definitely shouldn't rely on her to do all your chores- even if she does work for you."

Amused that a teenager was lecturing me, I found myself waiting for Mika to continue her lesson on duty and responsibility. It was apparent our conversation was going beyond the care of flowers; and in a way, she reminded me of Aunt May who also thrived on teaching me life lessons.

"I just don't understand why people decide on something and then just assume that there'll always be someone else to clean up their mess. It's like that for practically everything."

"Actually, it depends on what it is," I challenged back. "There are things you shouldn't neglect, but there are other things that aren't as important. For the less important things, you can get help or leave alone for awhile until you're done with the critical stuff in your life first."

Not at all impressed, the girl replied, "See? That's why all of you are so complicated. If you just made up simple rules, then everything wouldn't have to be this messed up."

It was insight I never expected from someone as young as Mika. But perhaps with whatever she had already experienced in this still-green life of hers was what made her just the right person to teach this lesson because there was an element of truth to what she just said. Perhaps life wasn't as complicated as we all claimed it to be. Perhaps in an effort to make life less complex, we had in fact, made too many rules to follow and in the process created even more nets and traps to stumble into and eventually get stuck. I had forgotten that life was only as complicated and frustrating as we let them be. The situations in our days were lifeless; while it was the people in them who made events happen. Had we all forgotten who controlled the script?

Tangled in my own web of hypocrisy, I was at a loss for words, knowing Mika was right. Satisfied that I couldn't retaliate anymore, the girl finished watering my plants and threw the hose at me in a surprise game of catch.

"Next time you do this job. These plants are yours."

Before letting her leave, I asked, "Can you at least remind me when I need to water them?"

Like a boy about to receive another scolding from his mother, I cringed in smug embarrassment and quickly added, "Just in the beginning. I need time to get into the habit."

Deciding it was a reasonable request, she nodded and continued on towards the house.

Left alone with my plants, I stared out into the open space of all the colors my garden had created through its own doing. I found myself almost ashamed to stand in front of something I claimed to be my own and yet had not spent one day to take the time to understand and nurture them. With this sudden perspective, I vowed to turn a new leaf and promised that I would be my garden's keeper. I only hoped this new abundance of life would give me another chance to protect them under my care.

*

With Henry and Mrs. Li not joining us for dinner that night, this left simply two people eating peacefully together. I was no longer babysitting a hostile snake but instead had taken in a girl who had gotten lost and was on a path of finding her way.

Mika began the conversation at the dinner table with the most unexpected question.

"So what did you and Steve talk about when he came?"

In awe, I asked, "How did you know he was here? He told you?"

In a matter of fact way, she picked at her food while replying, "No, I was in my room when I heard him and was just wondering why nobody told me. By the time I came out, both of you were gone."

"I thought you were sleeping and told him to come another day."

Still unsatisfied, she pressed on asking, "You had to say all that outside the house?"

Mika was proving to be an interesting subject to study. While it was something I could not see at first, this girl had an impressive inborn wit. Anyone wanting to strike up conversation with her would have to be alert and sharp. Though at times a mad tyrant beyond control of even the mightiest power; once settled, she had a calm about her that would draw anyone near just to bask in her presence. I was beginning to realize Mika had an inner substance few people had, and it was something worth respecting. It was a shame I didn't discover this sooner under all the anger she carried when she first walked through my door.

"It was pretty late when he came so I thought I would just give him a ride back home," I explained.

Growing impatient, Mika replied, "Yeah, I know all that. But what did you guys talk about after you left here?"

Suddenly feeling a little mischievous and wanting to show off my own wit, I teased with a smile, "You should have asked that in the first place."

Met with annoyance, I settled down like a child who had been given a warning from his mother, and morphed back into an adult once again.

"Okay, okay, I just asked really general questions…like his family and how he got to know you."

Turning back into a typical teen, her eyes rolled back in disbelief of the embarrassment I must have caused her as she imagined how our conversation could have gone in that car. I quickly assured her my questions were merely to break an awkward moment of silence and was not meant to make the boy uncomfortable or threatened.

This seemed to satisfy Mika as she turned her attention back to the food in front of her.

But now it was my turn to ask the questions.

"So, how did you meet Steve?"

Without looking up, she replied sarcastically, "I thought you asked him that already."

"I know…but I forgot what he said," I lied.

"School," was her simple answer.

Though curious and wanting to pry deeper, I stopped myself short detecting Mika's impatience. Like a child dodging a parent's inquiry, the girl was not keen on chatting anymore. I gave in and stopped talking as I silently reminded myself that there was always tomorrow.

Lesson 10: Grasp Hope Amidst Fear

Another dreadful day at work had passed. The meetings were finally over and our demanding clients had at last left the building. Even my hardworking assistant Nancy was slowly wearing away into exhaustion. I found myself feeling as though I had been beaten to a pulp as I packed up my things to call it another end to a stressful day.

Making my way down the hall towards the elevators, I suddenly heard Nancy holler my name in the distance, willing me to stop in my tracks. Turning back and curious of what else wouldn't let me go home and hide from the world, I waited patiently for Nancy to catch up to me.

As she approached, I saw worry in her eyes and grew fearful of what would come next. As though bracing me for a vicious fall, Nancy began carefully.

"Hospital from Main Street just phoned. They say that your Aunt May is in the hospital. You better go and see her now."

I felt myself freeze while desperately wishing that Nancy was playing a cruel prank, though I knew she would never do such a thing. There was no way that my Aunt May would be in the hospital when she was supposed to be on a cruise enjoying every luxury life could offer. Since the day

Aunt May left, there had been no reports of a cruise ship accident of any kind on the news. This had to be a mistake.

'May' was such a common name; the hospital must have contacted the wrong person. Tomorrow morning I had to remember to file a complaint to the hospital for making such a serious fault.

I was about to remind Nancy that Aunt May was on vacation and that there was no way she would be in the hospital, when she shook her head saying the doctors would explain everything once I got there.

Pushing me through the door, she shoved a piece of paper that had the hospital's address in my numb hands and set me free into a place where a new nightmare would soon begin.

*

Still in a daze, I got to the hospital and asked reception where I could find a patient named May Lam. As the nurse searched her files, I prayed desperately hoping she would look up from her computer with a puzzled look to tell me there was no such person taking up residence in their ward.

But instead, she directed me down a hallway that was shielded away from the commotion in the front and left me by a room where an old lady laid inside- frail and weak. She was stripped of most of her hair and emaciated with her eyes sunk so deep inside her skull, they were like two black holes.

Although weak, the old lady was still alert and gathered all the energy she could to struggle a smile my way. She was telling me not to be afraid and to come in.

But I was scared of this woman lying almost lifeless on the bed. I didn't know her and didn't want to know her. This woman did not have vigor or zest. She had already been robbed of life and was now only left with the remains of a weak spirit that would also abandon her all too soon. She was not my Aunt May.

And yet, with each step ventured towards this frail thin body, there was a spark that was still there, defiant and refusing to wither away. The dimples in an already beaten smile I always adored and defined as Aunt May was still alive. It was at that moment I couldn't deny that the person lying ever so fragile in front of me was the woman whom I cherished like a mother; and tonight she was going to leave me forever.

Too weak to speak, she beckoned for me to sit down. I obeyed and waited for what would come next.

Still smiling, Aunt May began in her broken English that I so adored. "Look like Aunt May will see Isaac's mom soon. If I know sooner, I should tell her to prepare room for me upstairs," she croaked weakly, staring up at the ceiling as though my mother's spirit was already there waiting.

Seeing that I wasn't amused of her humour, she sighed and patted my hand in comfort. I still kept quiet waiting for the explanation I deserved.

"Aunt May's life always crazy, but I never lie to you. This time I break rule."

Unable to contain my silence any longer, I cried out, "But why this time? You lied to me from the very beginning. You were never on a cruise. You knew you were sick and lied about it. Of all the times, why didn't you let me help you this time?"

Wanting answers, I let grief overwhelm me as tears spilled from my eyes. I ignored them, too scared to do anything with each passing moment. Time was so precious now, I didn't want it to move, yet was powerless from preventing it to do anything else.

Serene and calm, despite my panic, Aunt May began to speak again and called a name that only she could use- her smile never leaving her. "Ah-Hon...Isaac...Aunt May have to say something before she go. You be good boy and listen, okay?"

Willing to do anything that would make her happy in what little time we had, I nodded and clenched her hand even tighter as if letting go would mean losing her forever.

"Aunt May talk to your mom in dream long time ago. We both think you not happy. Back in village, me and your mom always poor. Always have to work hard and get yelling from other people but we always happy because we have free spirit."

Pausing to catch her breath, I waited in anticipation for her to begin again.

"Isaac, just like your father. Very hard working… but your mom come to Aunt May when Aunt May is sleeping and say she very mad at herself for not teaching her son how to live life. She come in my dream to ask me to help you. Ai ya…Isaac's mom and me are like sisters. I treat you like my son, of course I help lah. Even if Aunt May have to use own life to help you, I say 'yes'."

Another pause of breath.

"Isaac mom so smart. She tell me if Aunt May want to help Isaac, Aunt May need to get sick and use my life to save you. Ai ya…Aunt May already so old and already live a lot. I miss your mom and want to live with Heaven Emperor too. So I say 'okay', and get her to make me sick to help Isaac."

I was quite certain that at this point, Aunt May was delusional. While not much of what she relayed made much sense, I let her continue, and silently scolded myself for not listening to Aunt May more often in her healthier days.

But all the regret in the world would not matter now. With eyes blurred from silent sobs, I looked up at Aunt May pleading, "You'll be okay Aunt May. My mom won't let you die. She knows I still need you to take care of me."

Shaking her head, Aunt May replied, "You right...Aunt May don't die as long as you remember what I teach you in living world. If you listen what Aunt May teach you, me and your mom will follow Isaac all the time- even when we not in this world."

Not wanting to hear another word that hinted death, yet knowing that Aunt May needed to finish her story, I lowered my head in silence, allowing her to go on.

"After your mom come visit me in dream, I go to doctor and he say 'stomach cancer.' Already in final stage and cannot do anything. At same time I find out Mika need someone to take care of her. See? It is all Isaac's mom's plan. Even in heaven she is so smart. Plan everything good."

Heaving another exhausted breath, she continued on, "I send Mika to you so she can teach you things Isaac's mom forget to teach Isaac. Aunt May try to teach you too but run out of time now. Mika still young have lots of time."

Confused and a little delusional myself, I asked with a quivering voice, "What is it that you want me to learn Aunt

May? I promise you, you just have to tell me and I'll do whatever you want as long as you don't go."

Giving my shoulder a weak squeeze, she replied, "Silly boy. Die is last step in life. You supposed to be happy for Aunt May. Life is finally finished and I can enjoy more things in heaven with your mom. But what Isaac need to learn is not like learning about real estate and money. For Isaac, it is a lot harder than work things."

She paused then, taking a longer time to gasp for air before continuing. Her breath was growing increasingly shallow and I wanted to ask her to stop, even for a moment to rest. But I knew better and waited patiently for her to continue despite knowing how painful it was for her to muster every word. This was her last gift and likely the last advice I would ever receive from Aunt May.

Struggling with whatever breath she had left, Aunt May said in a feeble whisper, "You supposed to learn how to be happy. If you don't be happy even if Heaven Emperor give you 100 years life, you still like dead anyways."

And as I savoured those words, Aunt May's eyelids drooped as though freeing herself from life. My hysterical cries begging her to stay while yelling for anyone to stop Aunt May from leaving me were met with a smile still so delicately etched and warm on her face, even in the face of death.

*

"She's one tough cookie," were the doctor's comforting words as he stepped out of the room. They were simple words, but it was enough. Just now, Death had arrived, but my Aunt May held on. I knew she wasn't ready to go.

Hearing those words, I nearly melted onto my knees at the doctor's feet, thanking him with all my heart. He gave a strained smile and a pat on the back willing me to carry on. We both knew Aunt May had won a battle tonight, but she would eventually lose her war. Even so, it would not be tonight.

"You can go in and see her, but let her rest a bit. It's been a rough night for her. We've increased her drug dosage to ease the pain, but that's as much as we can do for her now. She's too far along, so chemo won't help. All we can do is wait and keep her comfortable. You understand, son?"

I nodded without saying a word, my mind yearning only to be by Aunt May's side and nothing else. The doctor eventually left but not before instructing me to let the nurses know if I noticed anything that needed attention throughout the night. I told him I would and headed back inside the room where I needed to be.

Once again, I saw a fragile woman now buried under tubes and an oxygen mask. Unlike before, I was no longer afraid and had to hold myself back from running over and hugging her with everything I had. I remembered what the doctor ordered and took my place in the chair next to her as I placed her thin hand in mine watching her rest.

Aunt May did not stir and I found myself monitoring her intently to make sure she was still breathing. So long as her heart was still beating, there was still hope. And it was with this hope that stayed with me throughout the night as I surrendered to sleep, resting by Aunt May's bedside guarding her from Death should it show its ugly face again.

I awoke to a gentle hand on my arm and raised my head to see Nancy who was relieved to find Aunt May and I resting peacefully together. Soon after, Aunt May began to stir and her eyes opened, ready to receive the world once again.

Seeing both of us by her side, she managed a weak smile and asked Nancy to come closer. She did as she was told and reached over to give Aunt May a hug while taking a seat next to me.

"This is a boring place for a vacation isn't it, Aunt May?" teased Nancy. I could always count on sweet Nancy to say the right thing at the right time.

Aunt May, always mischievous- even in sickness, responded back with, "Ai-yo…always do same thing on holiday, so I do something different this time mah."

And now with more concern, Nancy asked, "How are you feeling Aunt May? Are you feeling any pain? Do you need us to up the dosage on the drugs?"

Sinking back into the bed, Aunt May shook her head and said, "No, lah..just right. Why you both here? No work?"

To that question, both looked at me as I shook my head in response before asking Nancy how Mika was doing. She assured me Mika was fine and that Henry had taken her to school this morning. Hearing of Aunt May's condition, Mika wanted to visit, but Mrs. Li had convinced her school first and then visiting rights would come later. I was beginning to see that I was in fact blessed with kind and caring people in my life; but it was a shame that it had to take such a great tragedy for me to realize it.

Nancy reported she had already alerted people in the office of my absence and reminded me that the bulk of the work on our major projects was already complete. The tasks that remained were just follow up documents and calls needing to be done- all of which the staff were more than capable of accomplishing.

With Aunt May in bed listening intently, Nancy instructed that my main priority now was to be with my family. She would help take care of the rest.

Before I could thank her for her diligence, Aunt May jokingly asked, "Isaac, how come you never tell me Nancy get promotion?"

As both Nancy and I gave her a puzzled look, she continued on, "She is your boss now."

All of us chuckled- but not before Nancy's reply with, "And Isaac also forgot to mention he was going to give me a big raise too."

In between our jokes and laughter, a nurse came into the room to check on Aunt May. As the drug dosage, blood pressure and everything else was inspected, a thought came to mind.

After the nurse left, I turned to Aunt May and asked, "Aunt May, the doctor said that chemo is no good for you. If that's the case, why don't we get you out of here and have you come live with me? At least it'll be home and you'll be more comfortable."

Like a child who had just been offered free ice cream and candy, Aunt May eagerly nodded her head and shooed me out of the room to begin the paperwork that would get the process started. Her excitement made me move quicker as I rushed into the hall searching for her doctor to bring Aunt May back home with me.

I finally found him and pitched my proposal. He agreed that it was a good idea, as long as the patient would come back to the hospital if the cancer turned for the worse. I gave him my word and promised Aunt May would receive the premium care she needed back at home. Knowing that she would be in the capable hands of Henry and Mrs. Li, I knew Aunt May would be well looked after even if I was working.

Everyone was so excited when I relayed the news later that day to the people at home. Though surprised, I was touched of Mika's great concern for Aunt May. She made sure that Aunt May's room was in top notch condition as she helped Mrs. Li clean and clear the area for the large bed that was to be her main place of rest. I had also gotten a wheelchair for Aunt May and couldn't help but smile watching the Li's and Mika practice together on how to work the apparatus so that anyone of them could tend to Aunt May when needed.

The day finally came when everything was prepared and Aunt May was freed from her hospital chains to come home with her family. In anticipation of this day, Aunt May's health had improved quite a bit and even requested a lower dosage of pain killers claiming that leaving the hospital was giving her a natural high.

The nurses, pleased of her enthusiasm and refreshed energy, listened to her request, but armed me with some extra pills in case the pain got worse at night. I thanked them for their kindness and wheeled my Aunt May into the sunshine with Nancy and Mika on either side of me. As we helped Aunt May into the car, I found myself completely and utterly content.

Lesson 11: Amend Regrets

I couldn't remember a time when my house was filled with this much laughter and life. There were still many weeks left, but it felt as though Christmas had arrived. Even in her condition, Aunt May brightened everything around her and in the course of doing so, gave all of us a reason to smile. That was the gift of Aunt May.

There were good and bad days as the cancer continued to poison her body. She was constantly in pain but refused to soak in anymore drugs than needed, insisting that we were her pain killers. No matter how fierce the hurt, and how great her exhaustion, Aunt May's smile was always there to greet us. So long as we were by her side, she didn't need anything else.

I found myself growing more and more fearful of losing her. Behind my confidence and assurances that Aunt May still had plenty of time with us, I knew it wasn't true. In fact, I think everyone knew it was only a matter of time before our sweet Aunt May would be taken from us, and this time we would not be able to get her back. But until that day came, we were all determined to safeguard life in the house, hoping that Death would delay its pick up a little while longer.

For me, I couldn't remember the last time I worked late. I wasn't afraid of the end of a work day anymore because I knew there were people waiting for me to come home. These days, the minute I stepped in the office, I found myself waiting impatiently for time to pass so that it would free me back to the people I cared about.

And every night, Aunt May would be there waiting for me. There were many days when I found her with Mrs. Li in the kitchen as they exchanged stories of the hardships they had to endure back in their home villages. Other times, she would be with Mika in the living room either watching television or be playfully arguing with Mika of how "uncool" or "awesome" the latest fashion trends and movies were, as though she was a teenager all over again.

And when these moments tricked us into believing that perhaps Aunt May was defeating her disease, the pain would return reminding us not to be so naïve. When it got to be too much to bear, she would retreat to her bed and nurse the hurt by reading a book or simply succumbing to sleep. No matter where she was or what she did, Aunt May never let go of her smile and would cast an even brilliant grin as I came home every night. She was always eager to hear how my day went.

It was like this for some time, until one day when Henry picked me up from work, I noticed him driving a little quicker than usual. Before I could ask what was wrong, he reported that Aunt May's pain had returned- but this time, with a vengeance. While everyone could see Aunt May wince and hear muffled heaves of a woman in torturous pain, she had refused to go to the hospital insisting it would pass like all the other times.

When we arrived home, grimness had already invaded every inch of space in the house. Mrs. Li confirmed her husband's report, but surprised me by saying Aunt May was sitting out on the balcony.

Dropping everything, I quickly made my way outside and saw Mika. Without a word, she shuffled pass me, sulking and with tears glistening in her eyes. Though puzzled, I continued swiftly ahead while reminding myself to see the girl afterwards. I found Aunt May in her wheelchair soaking in the sunshine and light breeze that had decided to come for a visit.

She gave her usual smile as I pulled up a chair beside her, anxious to hear how she was doing. Patting my hand, Aunt May turned my palms up towards her and placed a locket inside it.

Met with a questioning look, Aunt May leaned back into her chair and said, "Aunt May tell you something, okay?" Though she was exhausted and I wanted for her to rest more than anything else, I knew better than to resist and let her say what she wanted to share.

"Since last time in hospital when I almost go to heaven, I think lots. I confuse why I didn't go. When Aunt May's heart stop for a bit, I see Isaac's mom, and ask her to take me, but she only say 'no'. When I ask her why, she say I still have one more thing to do."

"You have many more things you need to do, Aunt May," I responded firmly. "It's just not your time yet…not for a long while."

Smiling, Aunt May replied, "Isaac half right. It's not Aunt May time yet. But it is coming soon because I already finish what your mom want me to do."

"What else could mom ask you to do? " I asked, baffled. "You've already given your life."

"Ah…," she responded knowingly. "This time not about Isaac, but about Aunt May."

"I'm not sure what you mean," I replied slowly.

Settling back further in her chair, Aunt May began, "When Aunt May and your mom grow up in village back home, we very poor. Always hungry and cold because not enough food or clothes to wear. Aunt May and your mom very good friend like sisters, but we are very different. Your mom always good girl. Don't want much in life. She even think that if she stay in village until die, then that is no problem. She always think as long as she marry good man and have good kids, then life good."

Pausing to catch her breath, Aunt May continued, "But Aunt May not so good girl. I remember Aunt May's dad always hit her because he say she has too much wild blood. If he doesn't hit it out, Aunt May will always be a bad girl. It's true. Aunt May always think that better life will happen outside village and try to think of lots of ways to go away. Aunt May's wild blood is always inside her, even after beating and even when she grow up. Later, I meet very handsome man when I was young woman and think he will take me out of village because I think he loves me and will do what I want. Handsome man was good person, so Aunt May marry him, but he also is like your mom. He only want to stay in village and have babies with Aunt May. Ai yo…Aunt May so young, don't want baby, but think maybe if she have one baby for husband, he will take them out of village."

"I have one baby boy. He very cute and handsome like father. I think 'okay, now we can all leave village'. But Aunt May's husband only want more baby and want to build bigger house in village. Lots of fighting and crying. I feel very bad for myself and don't want husband or new baby anymore."

Aunt May was developing a cough. As I patted her back in hopes of soothing her, I suggested we head back inside for her to finish her story. But she refused, asking me to let her continue. I gave in once again. Little did Aunt May know, I was growing curious of where her story was leading.

"So, one day when son and husband sleeping, Aunt May leave in secret. She buy one way ticket to big city and just go because she can't live in little village anymore. Ai yo….if Aunt May can go backward and choose again, Aunt May will choose to stay with son and husband forever."

"When Aunt May come to big city, life also very hard. Everything so noisy and loud, but Aunt May like noise. Only night time, when very quiet make Aunt May cry, because she miss son and husband. Aunt May drink lots to try and forget, but it doesn't work. Aunt May want to go back home, but know everyone in village must be very mad at Aunt May and don't want Aunt May back. So time pass fast in big city. Aunt May lucky to get good job in office and lots of men want to marry Aunt May. But Aunt May say 'no' to everyone. In my heart, I am still marry woman and still miss my son, even if my son don't know me anymore."

Tears were forming in Aunt May's eyes as I once again put a comforting arm around her as though my hug would relinquish all the guilt she had for the family she abandoned. It was now clear why as a boy I would notice Aunt May looking at me so intently as though wishing for a miracle. I now understood that what I saw was a mother longing for her child and husband.

I felt pity for Aunt May and said, "It's okay Aunt May...all of that is in the past. If you like, we can go back to the village and try to find your family. So much time has passed; maybe they've already forgiven you. I'm sure your son would want to know what his mother is like."

Shaking her head in between silent sobs, Aunt May replied, "No lah...too late. My son and husband already gone."

"What do you mean gone, Aunt May? Were you able to contact your family back home?"

Nodding her head, she answered, "After live in big city a few years, Aunt May see your mom again at Mah Jong party. Your mom so good memory, still recognize me. Make Aunt May even more bad person because I almost don't recognize her. She marry your dad back in village and your dad move you and your mom to big city after Isaac born. He think that big city will give Isaac better life than small village."

"Ai-ya...when I hear this, I feel Heaven Emperor play trick on me. I think I learn new word...call something...ironic...I think so much and so hard to get out of village and your mom don't care. In the end, she get to live life that Aunt May want and Aunt May have to live in shame."

"Did mom and dad already know what happened with you?" I asked.

"Aunt May very ashame in beginning, don't know how to explain. But your mom and dad already hear something about Aunt May back in village. So I tell them everything and think for sure Isaac's mom and dad don't want me for friend anymore. But they surprise me and say they see me after all these years so far away from home. It is fate. Your mom say I always good big sister to her and know that I will be good Aunty to Isaac."

"So, did mom or dad get you in touch with your family?"

"Yes…I never ask, but Isaac's mom know I regret come to big city by myself. She know I miss my baby and husband very much. But Aunt May don't have baby anymore. Baby is now a boy. Isaac's mom talk to her family in village and ask for pictures of Aunt May's son and family. She pretend that she want picture to show to Isaac, but give pictures to me every time and tell me how life is for my husband and son."

Ever the more curious, I pried, "How was life for them when you left?"

Lowering her head, in disgrace she replied, "I hear husband not same after I leave. Very sad all the time. My son grow up in very sad home and always very serious and sad like his dad. He grow up and then marry a woman in village. But she just like Aunt May- a very bad woman. He don't want to be like his dad, so he listen to her and move into big city. But wife still not happy. After having baby in big city, she leave with another man."

I was growing suspicious with each word Aunt May shared, but remained quiet, patiently waiting for her to finish her story. I wanted to hear the ending to see whether the grand finale of her sad tale would confirm what I was beginning to suspect.

"So like his father, my son have to take care of baby girl all by himself with no wife and very sad all the time too. Finally, my son die from being too sad too long. Aunt May hear all this from another Mah Jong friend and cry for so many days because I don't see my son since he was baby, and now he die and I still don't see him. Aunt May so angry at herself. But I remember I have grand-daughter now. She still young, still need someone. So, I find information and go to her and pretend I am old family friend because I know she will also be mad at me if she know who I really am. At the same time, Isaac's mom come visit me in my dream and ask for my help. Isaac is like my son too, so I say 'yes'. I say that maybe my grand-daughter and Isaac can meet and help each other. Your mom think it is also very good idea..."

"And your grand-daughter is Mika." I said flatly.

"Ah…Aunt May know Isaac is very smart boy," as she nodded her head weakly.

"Aunt May don't plan to tell Mika, even if I die. I see Mika so good now and think she better not to know. But your mom come that day at the hospital and tell me I can't lie anymore. If I keep lying, then bad luck will go to Mika and she will be just like my husband and my son. I don't want to make more mistake, so I know I have to tell her."

And as though stating the obvious, I looked up at Aunt May and said, "When I saw Mika just now, did you already tell her the truth?"

Aunt May nodded and sighed, "When I tell her, she don't say anything- just cry. When she hear you come back, she say she have to go to room."

"And what is the locket for, Aunt May?"

"Locket is for Mika…inside is picture of Mika's dad and mom. Even though not here anymore, she still need to know where she come from. I know Mika will always be mad at me, but Aunt May want Mika to know she have family and her family love her very much."

Aunt May let out another exasperated sigh. It was as though she was finally able to breathe freely again after all these long years of guilt and regret. She was no longer imprisoned by fear and had finally come to terms with her wrongs.

As I wheeled Aunt May back into the house, I promised her I would make sure the locket would be returned to its rightful owner.

MIKA

Lesson 12: Learn To Forgive

I don't know why I even bothered trying. I was such an idiot to think that maybe my life was turning itself around. I should have known better than that. Good things only happen to other people- but never for me. That woman had dropped a bombshell on my world and demolished everything I knew about me- inside and out.

That is what Aunt May did to me. Aunt May....or was it *grandma*...?

Ugh...I could not believe that all this time, she had made me believe she was just Aunt May who was my granddad's old friend...it was a sick joke.

When she told me about dad- her son and what she did when she was young, I couldn't think of anything else but wrap my hands around the old lady's neck and squeeze all the little life that was left of her. It was because of her I never had a real dad, or parents for that matter. I was too young to even remember what mom looked like when she ditched us. Growing up, when everyone had overprotective dads who drove them to school or to the malls, I was left to walk home by myself everyday to a place where a depressed man sulked and rotted away into nothing.

I remember dad lying lifeless on the couch day after day and had wished he was an alcoholic or someone who abused his kid to let out whatever it was killing him inside. At least that would have been *something*. Instead, he did nothing but live inside his own bubble of shame, missing his unfaithful wife and regretting everything he ever did in his life. He completely forgot that he still had me who needed love and affection.

If Aunt May had ignored her selfishness and just focused her life on being a good wife and mom, my dad would have never followed in his dad's footsteps and turn into the pathetic man that he was. I was sure of it.

This woman screwed up my life even before I was born; and if that wasn't enough, she had just taken away what little security and sense of identity I had left- just so she could go away in peace. After all these years, she was still the same selfish bitch.

These thoughts went around in my head over and over again as Aunt May's confession kept echoing inside my ears. I was so mad- it was beyond anything I had ever known. But at the same time, I couldn't help feel a sense of relief to know that I at least still belonged to someone. She was in fact my grandma and a part of her would always be stuck to me, whether I liked it or not. I wouldn't admit it to anyone, but a part of me was thankful that she had chose to finally tell the truth before it was too late for her…for us.

I dunno…maybe it was her twisted way of giving me a good-bye gift by telling me that I was not alone. Whatever it was, I now had something I thought I would never be able to have- a family. But I couldn't just forgive, and accept what had just been given to me. That would be too easy for someone who had done so much wrong. It wouldn't be fair for me to just take her back into my life just because she was ready now. Doing that would make her think I was a pushover, when I wasn't. I wasn't going to be a pushover for anyone.

But I couldn't think anymore with someone knocking on the door. I wait for a few more knocks before deciding to answer it. I knew it would probably be Isaac anyways.

*

ISAAC

This was more than what I had bargained for. When I took in Aunt May, I was fully prepared to be her caregiver, but not her family mediator and certainly not a counselor to her grand-daughter. But this was exactly what I was going to be doing.

After settling Aunt May in her room and reassuring her over and over again that I would go check in on Mika as soon as I could, I found myself lost. Nothing could help me understand the turmoil that had just hit Mika. I didn't know how to tell her that things were still alright. The thought of approaching the girl frightened me, knowing Mika's temperament and the crazy she was capable of.

At that moment, I did the only thing I could think of and called Nancy. I needed her insight, if only to hear her soothing voice and reassurance that everything would eventually work out.

She was still in the office when I called her. Despite the fatigue in her voice, Nancy quickly grew concerned knowing I was calling about Mika.

I gave a brief synopsis of Aunt May's story as she listened quietly and in shock.

"Wow," said Nancy after I was done.

"Yeah, I know right? So I have this locket with me now, but don't know how to give it back to Mika. To be honest, I'm a little scared. You know how crazy she can get."

"Well, I'm sure if she was going to do something stupid, she would have done it a long time ago. But you said she went right to her room and she's been pretty quiet ever since. The fact that she didn't storm out of the house and make you look for her tells me she's more mature than what we give her credit for."

Once again, Nancy's simple words gave me the greatest comfort and the courage to move forward with the dilemma as I replied, "Good point...so what do you think I should do now?"

"Knock on her door and see how she is. I'm sure you'll know exactly what to do once you see her."

They were few words with little instruction, but it was enough to calm my nerves. Grateful my trusty assistant had once again gone above and beyond her call of duty; I thanked Nancy and promised that I would report back to her after talking with Mika.

Venturing down the hall towards the girl's room, I sucked in a deep breath and clenched my fist before knocking gently on her door. At first, there was no response as I knocked again, growing a little anxious and hoping Mika didn't do something insane within the confines of her own silence.

But all fear was put aside as I finally heard shuffling and sniffling before she opened the door letting me into her world that had just been knocked off balance again. It looked as though Mika had been crying, and as I stepped inside her room, I offered a small smile and asked softly, "How are you doing?"

Giving her nose a quick rub, the girl gave a cold shrug and replied, "What do you think? I always thought I had a tramp for a mother and a loser for a dad. But now, it turns out I have to deal with a grandma who ditched my dad when he was a baby. Moms ditching their kids run in my family…it's just great."

The girl's grim sarcasm couldn't help but make you pity her, though I knew better than to offer sympathy now. But before I could speak, Mika continued her rant as anger slowly escalated with each word. "I can't believe how selfish she is. Waiting until she's about dead to tell me. You know she only told me now because she doesn't want to feel guilty when she dies. If she wasn't dying, she probably would have pretended to be Aunt May forever. And now she wants me to forgive her after all that? She's got no right to ask for anything!"

I responded in Aunt May's defense. "I don't think she wants your forgiveness. I think she just wants you to know that you have family and that you're not alone. She told me that just now herself."

"Nobody bothered to ask if I wanted to know. She just went ahead and made the decision for me. Ugh….unbelievable!"

"Mika, I don't think you mean that," was my simple reply.

And with that response, I was met with silence. It was as though the girl had suddenly lost her steam. Releasing an exasperated cry, she plopped herself on the edge of her bed looking beaten and defeated.

"I know how angry you must be- and you have every right to be feeling the way you do. She should have told you who she was the first day she met you. But Aunt May had her reasons. You were a different person then. If she had shown up at your doorstep on the first day announcing that she was your grandma, you wouldn't have accepted her. You have to understand that."

"And now that she's sick, maybe you're right. Maybe it's her way of relieving some of the guilt, but I also believe that she regrets leaving her family. She was young and stupid then and couldn't think straight. By the time she knew she had made the wrong choice, she thought it was too late to turn back."

"That's not an excuse," Mika replied coldly.

"No, it's not, but it's what she felt at the time. And you can't change what happened in the past. Can you imagine the weight Aunt May must have been carrying all this time? She's been beating herself up alone, but at least she was finally brave enough to own up to her mistake and spoke up. You at least have to give her credit for that."

"Yeah…so now what? Does she expect me to run and give her a big hug and be her good grand-daughter now?"

"I told you that Aunt May doesn't expect you to forgive her. That never was her intention. She knew that by telling you who she really was, there would be a possibility she would never see you again. Do what you feel like doing. Talk to her or even yell at her if you want. But maybe turn your focus away from Aunt May and think about yourself for a bit."

Met with questioning eyes, I explained saying, "Forget about Aunt May and what she did and think only how you would be if you chose to ignore the fact that you have a grandma who loves you and is living right down the hall. Just think for a second, would it really be the end of the world if you accepted what you just heard for simply what it is."

Still silence.

"I'm not saying you have to forgive Aunt May for anything. In fact, you can keep holding a grudge against her forever- but that won't change the fact that she's still your grandmother. Which would let you be a happier person?"

"Neither would make me any happier," Mika pouted back. "If I forgive her, I'll still always think of how selfish she was for dumping my family. If I cut her off completely, I'll be just as pissed off and alone."

Lending a comforting hand on her shoulder, I responded gently, "Mika, Aunt May was a different person when she was young. If given the chance to do it all over again, she would have been the responsible adult. But that was in the past and can't be undone. She's already old and doesn't have much time left. It's now your turn to choose. You've being given a second chance and I don't want you to live with regrets like Aunt May."

With nothing else left to offer, I got up from my seat and headed towards the door, but not before saying, "When you're ready Mika, go see your grandma again. You don't have to hug or kiss her, just think of her as someone who screwed up, and then decide whether you can get to know her again."

Before clearing the doorway entirely, I heard Mika call out quietly, "Isaac…"

"Yeah…?"

"Thanks."

I turned back towards the girl and smiled replying, "No problem…and I really do think you should go see your grandma when you're ready. She has something to give you."

*

The house fell back into a silent vegetative state that night without Mika or Aunt May at the dinner table. Knowing Henry and Mrs. Li would be confused with the sudden change, I gave them the same synopsis as I did with Nancy to put their worries to rest.

I assured them that both women needed some time on their own to sort out the day's revelations. And knowing the strength both of them possessed, I knew they would be alright in time.

After dinner, I visited Aunt May again to see how she was doing. Despite her strength, today had taken a great toll on the woman leaving her utterly exhausted inside and out. But seeing me, she struggled to rise to a sitting position in her bed as I rushed to her side. Not wanting to waste another minute, she urged me to recite how my talk with Mika went.

I told her all that had happened, and shared what Mika had told me of her anger, disbelief and conflicting dilemma of not knowing what to do. I then relayed the advice I gave the girl and placed the locket back into Aunt May's hand.

Before allowing Aunt May to protest, I patted her arm saying, "It's not right for me to give this to Mika. Aunt May, you're her grand-mother and should be the one to give this to her."

Knowingly, Aunt May sighed sadly and nodded her head.

"Ai-yo…I want to…but she so mad. I don't think I see her again and don't have chance to give to her."

With a comforting smile, I replied, "I wouldn't be so sure yet. Give her some time Aunt May…you two are each other's family and family eventually forgives each other no matter what it is…."

That night as I retreated to my study to catch up on some reading, I heard a soft tap down the hall. After a brief moment of silence, a door gently opened and then closed shut again with the shuffling of timid feet. I let out a satisfied sigh and couldn't help but smile. The girl did have a heart after all.

Lesson 13: Good-byes

I wanted to see Aunt May before heading to work, when both Henry and Mrs. Li stopped me. Like children on Christmas morning, giddy and excited, they told me with big smiles that Mika was still in Aunt May's room.

"I think Mika in there whole night," reported Mrs. Li with a big grin.

And with an approving nod, Henry added, "We hear lots of talking…talk, talk, talk all night. Very good."

It was good news indeed.

I decided then to head straight to work knowing that Mika was with Aunt May. As I followed Henry out the door to the car, I found myself excited to get into the office. Being at work would mean seeing Nancy and I couldn't wait to share the ending of Aunt May's heartfelt story. I knew she was probably anxious to know how it ended herself.

Just as I predicted, no sooner had I settled in my office and powered on the laptop, there was a gentle tap on the door with Nancy peering in asking for answers.

I invited her to take a seat before recounting all that had happened the night before- including my talk with Mika, going back to Aunt May to convince her that the locket was for her to give, and how Mika decided late last night to give her grandmother a second chance.

Simply ecstatic after hearing my story, Nancy clapped her hands before jumping up exclaiming, "Excellent! This is definitely turning out to be a great day. The city just called and confirmed that the Capersville Building is officially free from asbestos and we are good to go for construction."

As Nancy continued on with the next steps of the project, I found myself thinking a little more about the Capersville Building. The structure used to belong to a well-known European tycoon- Victor Lasonce; and in its glory years stood tall and mighty in the downtown core with its modern offices and high-end shopping boutiques.

As the years passed, time- or rather Victor's corporation- decided it was no longer the sophisticated hub that the company once thought it was. Slowly, its businesses moved out of the building one by one until nothing was left except for a few convenience stores, mainly used as a last minute shelter or bathroom for the homeless. It had turned into a wasteland and would only be a matter of time before the entire building would be demolished and made into a parking lot.

But I saw something more. I remember the countless nights driving on Capers Street if only to pass by the building envisioning the potential it still had. I recall asking Nancy if she thought the structure was worth saving and was met with an encouraging smile urging me to begin the process.

That was five years ago. Five long years of first striking a business case to convince my company that Capersville still had hope and was not dead yet; followed by long dragged-out negotiations with Lasonce's group of buying the building and land that still belonged to Victor at the time; and then buying out the businesses that were still too stubborn to vacate the place.

And of course, I couldn't also forget the lengthy and strenuous process of applying for the required permits and going through the right bureaucratic channels with the city when entering into these kinds of rebuilding projects. Even with the political contacts I had managed to forge, it was still a constant struggle filled with obstacles of bureaucracy and angry, frustrated people. As if joining the bandwagon of bad fortune on this project, city inspectors had informed us a few months ago that there were suspicions of asbestos contaminating the building. If it were not for Nancy's persistent coaxing and constant reminders of the great potential the building had, I would have surrendered long ago.

And now, with all hurdles finally overcome, I couldn't help but to stop and rethink the fate of Capersville once again. Was it truly fit to be another corporate hub housing multi-million dollar companies? In its early years, the building had already seen the glamour and sparkle money could offer. In an age of rush and chaos, how much more glam could Capersville take before diminishing once again into a shriveled prune?

Too much work had gone into reviving this building with it risking a second death. Surely there was something more sustainable, more meaningful, than tearing this building down only to build another one. Despite all the work done so far, this project was no different than all the others we had taken on. At the end of the day, it was still an exercise of buying out the structure and its people to build something else for money. Maybe we could be different this time and do something worth being proud of for once. Perhaps Capersville was just the right place for this new venture.

Seeing my distraction, Nancy stopped and asked with a concerned look, "Isaac, are you alright?"

With a reassuring smile, I nodded and said, "I am, but I'm starting to think of a new direction for Capersville…"

With curiosity, Nancy responded, "Go on….What exactly are you thinking of?"

I took a breath to gather my thoughts and began my pitch.

"So, we both agree that Capersville has potential. It's in exactly the right location to be in the centre of attention and can be revived into being something great again- just like what it was back in the day. We both think that this building has something special going on…agreed?"

Nancy nodded, urging me to continue.

"So, if it really is special, why are we doing the same old thing we do all the time? Buying a building, tearing it down only to build another big business and in the process pissing off a whole bunch of people?"

"Because that's the business we're in…that's what you say all the time…," Nancy replied slowly, unsure where I was going with this and probably beginning to think that the stress was getting to me.

"Isaac, maybe you need to stop and slow down a bit…"

I held up my hand asking for her patience saying, "Just hear me out a bit longer Nancy…I'm thinking out-loud here, but I do have a point, I promise you."

Satisfied, Nancy allowed me to go on.

"I know everyone has worked really hard on this file. But I can't remember the last time I felt proud of what I did. This is just a job…but it wears you out. You're right, this is the business that we're in- it's all for the money. But what if we can think out of the box for a bit? Could we not do what we always do, but modify the project to make it more meaningful at the same time?"

I saw Nancy's eyes and ears perk up and knew I had said something right as I pressed on.

"Instead of making another building for corporations and businesses, why don't we build something else…like a community centre? I've seen lots of big metropolitan areas do this. It'll be like a centre for youths who just want to hang out and meet friends in a clean and safe environment. The square footage is also big enough to have a community garden. We could partner with the city on this and it'll be a shared project- good PR and business for all involved. What do you think?"

I anxiously waited for Nancy to process all that was just proposed. It certainly was a different turn than what was initially planned for Capersville, but I believed with all my heart now that this was the right direction. I had never felt such conviction- so much that it frightened me.

I continued to wait patiently as Nancy thought out-loud.

"Well, Capersville's certainly in a prime location. It'll be easy access for everyone who wants to use its facilities. And it'll definitely be something different to draw people's attention to our company- but I guess in a more positive way this time…."

"What kind of facilities were you thinking of?" asked Nancy.

"I'm not sure yet, but the land is big enough for us to build multiple levels, so one floor could have a gym and swimming pool. Another level could have a lounging area with different fast food and coffee shop type joints. We could design another floor that has community halls for people to use for their private functions and events. And outside will be a community garden. The difference though between this centre and all the others is that people using the facility can pay whatever they can or feel is fair. They don't even have to pay if they can't. Those who want to use the halls can do it by paying a small rental fee. But overall, the centre will rely on donations. It'll be a community centre sponsored by our company in partnership with the city. Something like this would look good on both us and the politicians."

With a smile, Nancy nodded and responded, "I think it could work. But convincing the guys up top will take some time and then we gotta deal with the city all over again. You ready for this?"

There was no time to lose. I turned to my laptop and responded with a grin from ear to ear saying, "I'm booking a meeting with the board right now. Get the rest of our team in the conference room so that we can start working on the business case ASAP."

As she bolted out of my office, Nancy said, "We'll be in the conference room in a few minutes. Oh…and Isaac…"

"Yeah..?"

"I think this will be your best project ever."

With Nancy's blessing, I grabbed the Capersville file and followed her out of my office, refreshed and excited.

This was going to be a wonderful day for all of us.

*

The good cheer continued on throughout the day. My team was injected with fresh energy as I told them about the new Capersville project. Aware that there would be numerous sleepless nights ahead, they were still pumped. I was comforted to see that like Nancy and I, they also believed in this new found direction and was completely committed.

I returned home to more happy laughter. Mrs. Li and Aunt May were both at the kitchen table making dumplings for the night's meal as they greeted me. It was such a joy to see Aunt May well rested and happy. I wanted to soak in the moment and willed time to stop moving for her sake.

Looking around but not seeing Mika, I grew curious and asked if they knew where the girl was.

Before Mrs. Li could answer, Aunt May beamed proudly, "My grand-daughter in room. So good girl…do homework."

We all exchanged warm smiles and nodded knowingly. Nothing more was needed to be said. Where there was once conflict and turmoil, now there was only comfort and self-resolved peace. But still, I had not seen Mika for the whole day and was curious.

I walked down the hall and knocked. A few seconds later, Mika answered the door and like a teenager with attitude that was all too familiar, asked impatiently, "Yeah…?"

For reasons I wasn't sure of, I suddenly grew shy and embarrassed, but knew it was too late to turn back. I cleared my throat, and casually said, "Umm…nothing…just wanted to say hi…since I hadn't talked to you since last night."

I should have known better than to undermine the girl's intelligence. She saw through my fib instantly and rolled her eyes.

"Oh geez Isaac…that's so lame. If you want to know if everything is alright with me and grandma, you just have to ask. See?"

And with that, she showed me the locket that was now hanging on her neck. After all these years the necklace had finally found its rightful owner and was being worn with pride. It was a great sight for all to witness.

And from a distance, both of us could hear Aunt May declare, "Yah…me and Mika like best girlfriends you know."

I let Mika return to her books and retreated to my study to begin working on the new Capersville file. Even after a hectic day at the office, I was still energized and was so very excited to work the many more hours needed for the sake of our new project.

After a skipped dinner and hours of intense concentration, I became no match for hunger and fatigue and surrendered to their powers. Taking a big stretch, I headed silently towards the kitchen and like a scavenger, looked desperately for food that I knew Mrs. Li would have left for me in the fridge.

Like a mad man just released from prison, I breathed in the sweet dumplings and devoured the food like a savage, surprising even myself of how hungry I was. With my hunger satisfied, it was now time to appease fatigue as I headed towards the bedroom, ready for a good night's sleep.

But before heading back to my room, I noticed the balcony light still on. Following the warm glow, I was surprised to find Aunt May in her wheelchair staring out in the darkness alone- her eyes wide open; her mind deep in thought.

I didn't want to disturb her, but the wind was turning ferocious. I needed to bring Aunt May back inside so that she wouldn't catch cold. Careful not to startle Aunt May, I laid a gentle hand on her shoulder and knelt by her side ready to coax her back in.

But it was as though she had been waiting for me to appear all night, and started to speak before I could say anything. "You and Mika same people you know. Both want happy but get lost…."

Wanting to suggest that we talk after she got some rest, I began to speak, only to see Aunt May raise her hand asking me to stop and listen. I relented and waited for her to continue.

"Lost is okay, you know…but not good if you pretend you know the way, because the more you pretend, the more you get angry. The more you get angry, the more you burn your spirit until you don't have anything anymore except old body. If you have body but no spirit, it is like a ghost- you have no life and no meaning. Aunt May already have life for a long time and now want to give my spirit to Isaac so Isaac can live happy life too."

Hearing these parting words, tears began to blur my vision once again. I raised my head and struggled a sniffle saying, "I won't know how to be happy without you, Aunt May."

Thrilled to hear this, Aunt May exclaimed weakly, "Ahhh… Isaac already learning. Everyone come into world by himself and leave this world by himself. So…no such thing like

Isaac can't live without Aunt May or Aunt May can't live without Isaac. We only think that because we are scare and selfish for ourself."

"What do you mean Aunt May, I don't understand?"

With a fond look in her eyes, Aunt May dried my tears with the magic touch of her wrinkled, emaciated hand asking, "Why Isaac cry?"

"I'm crying for you, Aunt May."

Shaking her head, she replied tenderly, "Ai-yo…silly boy…that not right. You not crying for Aunt May. You cry for yourself because you don't want to see Aunt May go. But Aunt May say many times that I want to go and see your mom and Heavenly Emperor. So see, Isaac is selfish man because he want to keep Aunt May."

I was brought to a new revelation that seemed too horrible to be true. Helplessly, I could only lower my head waiting for Aunt May to go on.

"But that's okay Isaac, because I know you care for Aunt May a lot. Nothing wrong to be selfish sometime to be happy, but Isaac have to remember to let other people be happy too. If Isaac can't sleep at night because of voice in your head, then there is something wrong…"

"Aunt May…I never wanted to make other people's lives miserable.."

"No, no, no lah…ai-ya…Aunt May dying and Isaac still don't listen good to me," sighed my Aunt. She had always been able to find humour in anything- no matter how morbid the subject. I remained silent trying ever so desperately to understand the lesson she was trying to teach me.

"What Aunt May saying is all the buildings you take apart and sell now… is Isaac happy? You don't have to answer because Aunt May know you are not. Then why do you keep doing that? Isaac always say 'no choice', but there is always choice. I see Isaac grow up from little baby boy to big man and I know what your problem is. Isaac's problem is you can't let go, like you can't let go of Aunt May now even though I almost have no more time."

Catching her breath for a moment of air, Aunt May pressed on, "Just like if you want to drink water, you have to pour out tea from cup first before you pour water in. Isaac's cup of tea already too full. You get mad because people don't let you earn more money, or you get mad because client is not nice and doesn't sign your contract, and you also get sad because you think you don't have friends. Ai yo…so many many full cups…"

Distorted was her analogy, but I was beginning to understand what Aunt May was trying to show me. If my life's sorrows were to be described by cups, then I indeed had many.

My cups were filled with everything that was dark and toxic. Somehow, I had grown into a cluttered mess and in the process, had missed the mark of what life was supposed to be.

To outsiders, I was a successful man with all the material luxuries life could give. But if they were to look closer, beyond the surface of clothes, house and cars I hid behind, they would only find scraps that wouldn't be fit enough to make up a decent man. Those who had been brave enough in the past to come close and truly see who I really was, had been attacked and viciously banished as I stubbornly convinced myself they were just too simple to understand someone like me. But the truth was that I was afraid to admit that I was a damaged man and had been broken for a very long time.

As I wheeled Aunt May back to her room for the night, I silently promised both of us that I would change. My only regret was that it had cost my beloved Aunt May her life.

*

"Isaac, Isaac!" were the terrified cries of Mika barging into my room the next morning, barely out of bed. I knew right away something was terribly wrong.

Ignoring her need for air, Mika stammered breathlessly, "G-g-grandma's….hardly breathing…We have to go to the hospital!"

I quickly bolted out the door straight to Aunt May's room with Mika close behind my heels. We saw both Henry and Mrs. Li already helping Aunt May from her bed as I grabbed the car keys. Amidst the panic, I felt a hand on my shoulder. Though weak and thin, it still had an authority I could not ignore, and it was commanding me to stop.

I looked over and saw Aunt May smiling as I instructed Mika to grab any coat or sweater she could find for her grandmother.

Ever so softly, but firm enough for all of us to hear, Aunt May commanded, "Ai-ya…everyone stop lah…by the time we go to hospital, Aunt May already gone. Let's stay here and say good-bye…ok?"

How could we deny the dying wish of someone so dear? With a defeated sigh, I slowed down, though Mika would not give in, forbidding her grandma to leave her. Remembering Aunt May's last lesson from the night before, I went against all instinct and asked Mika to stop and be with her grandma in this final moment of her life.

"What? Are you crazy?" exclaimed Mika, choking back tears as Aunt May beckoned her grand-daughter to come back to her side.

Putting up a brave face, I replied, "She's right Mika. We all knew this was coming and there isn't much time left. It would do her much better to just stay here and be by her side to the end. Henry, can you help us call the doctor and have him come over right away?"

With a sad nod, both Henry and Mrs. Li left the three of us alone together for the last time.

Knowing it was now a lost cause, Mika rushed to Aunt May's side and cried saying, "I just got to know you…you're not allowed to ditch me again!"

Stroking the girl's hair ever so tenderly, Aunt May responded gently, "Mika, such a brave and smart girl. When grandma first see Mika, she scared and mad…but now heart is all fixed and she is all better. Grandma very happy. Mika not by herself, she have Isaac and Nancy and Henry and Mrs. Li…just like family…right Isaac?"

Struggling a smile for her, I answered, "Yes, Aunt May, we're all family…"

Sobbing like a baby, Mika cried, "…but it won't be right without you…"

"Silly girl…you have to let grandma go now…grandma very tired and want to see your dad and grandpa. I hope they are like Mika and can forgive me too. Before grandma go, remember what you promise grandma yesterday?"

"I don't remember…."

"Ahh…but you have to or grandma will be very sad…Mika promise grandma that you will be good girl and have good life and always remember you have family that love you very very much, even if they are not with Mika. Tell me you remember?"

With sniffles and tears, Mika raised her head to face Aunt May and nodded promising, "I'll remember…"

As Aunt May continued to stroke her grand-daughter's hair with one hand, she turned to me sitting on the edge of the bed and with her other hand, held mine as tightly as she could. I'll never forget those eyes that embraced mine filled with so much love, concern and comfort. She knew I had finally understood her last lesson and with a draw of breath whispered, "It very easy…we all just let go…"

Casting her final blessing on all of us, I saw Aunt May leave this world joining my mother and her family who I knew were anxiously waiting for her. Even as Death claimed her, Aunt May's smile never left. I knew she was on her way to find a new happiness and nobody- not even Mika, had the right to stop her.

With one last sob, I got up from the side of the bed and crossed over to where Mika was. As I offered her a comforting hug, the doctor appeared at the doorway with both Henry and Mrs. Li behind him. One look of how serene Aunt May looked lying in bed, told them that nothing was needed to be done because Aunt May had already said good-bye. We could only take comfort knowing she was going to a place she had wanted to go to for a long time.

Still, follow up work was needed to signify the end of a magnificent life. The appropriate people with the appropriate authorities were called in to handle Aunt May's departure.

I called Nancy later that morning, telling her the sad news and told her I wouldn't be back in the office for the rest of the week. Also saddened by the turn of events, Nancy reassured me that all would be well at work. She urged me to take care of myself before reminding me to also keep watch on Mika. I promised I would do both and headed out the door to begin the inevitable process of arranging Aunt May's funeral with her grand-daughter.

From the moment we left the house that morning, all became a blur. I only remember that in the following days, Mika and I worked tirelessly together choosing flowers, and finding a suitable reception hall for a grand service that would satisfy Aunt May if she was still here. It was as if her spirit followed us wherever we went, offering advice on flower arrangements or softly asking whether the casket would be sturdy enough to carry her across the bridge to the afterlife where my mother would be waiting.

Our last task was an inspection of the burial site where Aunt May's final place of rest in this world would be. Since my mother and Aunt May were such close friends, it was only fitting to have her final resting ground beside my parents.

Approaching the graves of my mother and father, I was ashamed to see weeds invading the plot that was supposed to be their place of rest. It dawned on me that while I had been busy with life, I had neglected them here all alone-defenseless against the pollution and brown grass that was suffocating them even in death.

Like a child begging forgiveness, I knelt in front of my parents and kowtowed to them with a million apologies. I wished with all my heart that they were able to hear my sorries and regrets wherever they were.

Mika knelt beside me and began to pull the weeds that were contaminating their graves. Besides talking to shop vendors and offering comments on casket choices, the girl did not speak much these last few days, resigned to her own quiet thoughts.

But now she began to talk again asking, "Are we gonna lay grandma here?"

Plucking the dead grass with Mika, I nodded saying, "My mom and your grandma were like sisters. I think having her beside my parents would be what she wanted."

Once again, I heard Aunt May's soft voice echo in my ears convincing me that she knew what life was all about. In a way she did know what life meant- at least for her- and did all that she could to live it to the fullest. She accepted everything in it, whether good or bad because it was a life that she had chosen.

And so, with Mika by my side, we continued with the arrangements and five days later we officially laid my beloved Aunt May beside my parents, peacefully and with dignity.

Lesson 14: Learn To Let Go

Funerals have a way of making people think selfishly. As Aunt May was lowered into the ground, I felt a loss that was so great - even greater than when I saw my parents off. Perhaps at the time, I knew that even with my parents gone, I at least still had Aunt May looking after me. But now, with her gone too, who else did I have?

All these thoughts of self- pity were muffled as I only had to raise my eyes to see Mika sobbing silently. While not so long ago, we were strangers, then enemies and now turned friends, I came to realize that with Aunt May leaving us, we would not be alone. By letting go of her life, Aunt May had left behind the most precious gift so that we could all go on: each other.

The day ended with Nancy, Mika and I staggering back to my place in the comforts of Mrs. Li's carefully brewed soup made with love and care. It's been said that a picture is worth a thousand words. For the Chinese, when soup is brewed by someone you love, it is worth a thousand concerns. This is when you know you belong to the family.

All three of us gulped down the soup with all our hearts to Mrs. Li's delight. Not much was said as all of us were exhausted from the day's event. After the brief comments of how well organized everything turned out and how pleased Aunt May would have been, Nancy offered a helping hand to wash the dishes. She ended up offering more help to Mika and Mrs. Li later that night as they gathered what was once Aunt May's belongings and packed them away.

After a long day, I offered to give an exhausted Nancy a ride back home.

Normally, when it was just Nancy and I alone together, we would talk about work. Tonight was different though as we both sat in silence drinking in the soft rumbling murmur of the car's engine.

Breaking the quiet, Nancy asked, "Are you honestly alright? It's okay if you aren't."

"Don't worry, I'm fine. I admit I'm still in a bit of a shock, but everyone has their time. I'm just thankful that Aunt May went peacefully with not much pain in the end."

Relieved and comforted by my words, yet still not completely convinced she replied, "You're right that at least she went peacefully, but that doesn't mean you can't mourn for her though."

Met with my silence she continued on, "Actually on second thought, can you take me to a place before going home?"

We made the several turns she directed until we arrived at a deserted place to a blanket of blackness where the only noise was of the crickets playing Mother Nature's music. Baffled, I turned to Nancy waiting for an explanation.

Without a word, she motioned for us to get out of the car and beckoned me to follow her. We walked in darkness with the city buildings standing tall in the distance as I began to feel sand seep into my shoes. Still walking deeper into the night, I saw a rippling body of black that reminded me of sticky tar; and realized almost right away that it was actually a blanket of water shimmering under a moonlit sky.

"Umm…Nancy…why are we here?" I asked, though impressed with the beauty that surrounded us.

"When I was a kid, my family would come here once in awhile for picnics and stuff. Dunno why, but I always liked this place since it's kinda away from everything without you taking a plane."

Smiling, I replied, "You're still not convinced that I'm okay?"

Making herself comfortable, she sat down while running her fingers through the sand and answered, "Even if you were okay, I think I probably would have come here anyways by myself for a breather. It was a busy day. Besides, it's always nice to have someone with you for company."

I sat next to her and took my shoes off. Taking a deep breath, I released whatever worries and sadness I had inside of me and gave them back to the water. Whoever made night and day had an interesting concept. To think that with every sunset, history was made and with every rise of the morning light, the future would be in front waiting for us to walk the path we would choose to take.

My thoughts turned back to our most recent loss. With the rise of the morning sun, Aunt May's life was history while my life would continue to exist in the present and beyond. It was amazing that with just a simple sunrise, I would never be able to see or talk to Aunt May again. At the same time, the life ahead of me would still be a mystery until I took the next step. What was different before was that I always had Aunt May walking with me; whereas from now on, she would no longer be by my side to coach and mentor my every move. *God...how I missed my Aunt May.*

"You're so quiet, what are you thinking about?" asked a curious Nancy.

Digging my feet deeper into the sand and feeling the tiny pebbles between my toes, I shrugged my shoulders replying, "Just happy for Aunt May that she lived such an amazing life. She had her regrets, but in the end she owned up to them and left happy. Wonder when I die if I will be as carefree as she was."

Looking out into the water that lay in front, Nancy replied, "I don't think it's possible to go without any regrets. I'm sure your Aunt May had her moments too. But I think the difference is that she turned her regrets as a part of her life rather than obstacles."

Intrigued, I wanted to know more and asked, "Care to elaborate?"

With a smile, she answered, "All I'm saying is that people nowadays are so petty…almost wimpy. They can't seem to accept the fact that failure and regret is supposed to be what life is about. The moment they face something unexpected or unpleasant they see it as something they have to get rid of."

"What's wrong with that? To get to your goal you have to get past what's blocking you."

"You're right, nothing's wrong in trying to get past something in your way, but you have to remember life is a learning process too."

She continued on saying, "Take Mika for instance. A bright girl, but still so narrow minded. She's trying so hard to forget the guy who almost ruined her life, but she doesn't realize that the more she tries, the more difficult it is to get him out of her mind."

Instinctively, I defended Mika and challenged Nancy. "What should she be doing then? At least it's better than if she tries to get back together with him."

"I'm not suggesting that she should go and find him. But there's no need to force herself to forget the guy. The more she tries, the angrier and bitter she'll get- so much that she'll never be able to forget him."

As I paused in thought, Nancy took a handful of sand in her hand and squeezed it ever so tightly until it began to leak from her palms and trickle back onto the ground.

"It's just like what I'm doing now. I want to hold onto this pile of sand, so I squeeze it tightly. But if I hold onto it too tightly, in the end, all the pressure actually makes it slip right out of my hands."

"So what do you suggest?" I asked.

"I think Mika should accept the fact of what happened. She should learn to accept the mistake she made and turn it into a learning experience. She should always remember what attracted her to the guy in the first place. But whatever he did to hurt her, she should use it as a reminder for the next person she meets. That way, with each relationship she gets into, she'll learn something about herself until she knows exactly what she's looking for."

"Sounds reasonable I guess. Have you told her this?"

Nodding, she responded, "I have, but she still has to do one more thing."

"What's that?"

Turning to me, she answered, "Letting go."

Chuckling at the clever response, I nodded in agreement. Perhaps a part of Aunt May would always be here with us, forever reminding me that she was always right.

As we headed back to the car, Nancy added, "Funny how the older we get the more we're unwilling to let things go."

I couldn't agree with her more.

After seeing Nancy off and coming back to a quiet home, I felt empty all over again. While Aunt May had already been gone for five days, this was the first night since her passing that nothing was needed to be done. The service was complete; Aunt May's belongings were all taken care of; and even the lawyer had come earlier that day announcing everything that was stipulated in Aunt May's final will.

In it, Aunt May had listed all the various charities that her clothes and other such materials would be donated to. Through the years, she was a hard working woman and did well financially for herself. And while she would always carry a piece of regret and guilt for abandoning her family long ago, she did the next best thing for her only grand-child by leaving her a small fortune. The amount was enough to see Mika through college and beyond. But until the girl was old enough to access the money, I would oversee the funds and be her legal guardian. It occurred to me then that Aunt May must have had this arrangement all planned out long before I had even met Mika. Knowing she would soon be leaving us, she needed to be sure that we would all be taken care of once she was gone. *Sweet Aunt May…how I miss you…*

Down the hall, I noticed a dim light still glowing in Mika's room. At first unsure whether to leave the child in her peace or check on her, I decided to pay the girl a quick visit.

I knocked gently on her door before opening it ever so slightly and saw Mika in her bed mesmerized by the pictures in a photo album- locket in hand.

Breaking away from her intense concentration, Mika looked up to see me and then down again to the pictures without saying a word. I walked towards her and took a seat on the edge of the bed, curious of what she was doing.

"What are you looking at?" I asked.

"Grandma gave me this photo album a few weeks ago. These are the pictures she had of my family. I'm trying to look for one that has grandma in it so that I can put it in my locket."

"Doesn't the locket already have a picture of your parents in it?" I asked.

"Yeah...but I want to replace the picture with my dad and grandma instead..."

I didn't know what to say, but wanted to find some comforting words for a girl who had just lost the only family she had ever known. But before I was able to find the right words, Mika spoke again.

"My mom left us when I was a baby, so she's pretty much a stranger to me. I don't have really great memories of my dad, but at least he stuck around and didn't leave. Grandma is the only person in my family that I got to know a bit. So...I was thinking it would only be right to have her in the locket, especially when she was the one who gave it to me in the first place. It'll feel like she's always close by at any rate."

Without uttering another word, I took the photo album from her and sifted through the pages in hopes of finding something worthy enough to be a part of Mika's locket. Going through the pages of pictures, we saw what a miraculous life the woman had led. And while there were moments in her journey where darkness had haunted her, she had refused to surrender to its cruelty and lived on, making amends wherever she could. In the end, the life that was given to her was not wasted- and in fact had enriched the lives of so many others. I couldn't help but feel proud of this woman whom I called Aunt but was so much more to me than words could ever describe.

"Grandma must have been a really strong person," Mika said, looking at a picture with Aunt May smiling into the camera while sitting on the bus. She must have been going to work that day.

"She was," I replied. "Aunt May would always say to me that it was her choice to stay single. And because it was her choice, it meant she did have to be lonely at times. But in exchange, she got freedom and a life not many people from her home village could enjoy. She always said that once you made a choice, you have to live with all of it – good or bad. I always thought there was something more she wanted to tell me whenever she talked about not getting married. She always seemed sad and now I know why. She was of course thinking of you and your dad."

"Hmmm…what if the choices you made were wrong…? I wonder what grandma would say if she were here."

"Probably to try to fix it or work with it the best you can. I think she realized the big mistake she made after leaving your grand-father and dad, but couldn't do anything about it until it was too late."

"Yeah…what she did back then definitely was stupid," Mika responded knowingly.

"It's funny…Nancy and I were also talking about this sort of thing when I was driving her home."

"Yeah? What did she say?"

"Nancy said that we should take up whatever wrong choices we make and turn it into a lesson- because that's what life is- a learning process. We should pick out the parts of a choice that will help us grow and learn; and forget about the rest of the scraps and move on with life."

"What if you get stuck?"

Placing a hand on her shoulder, I answered, "I think that moving on is also a skill we need to learn. Some people are naturals and can do it no problem no matter what, but for others, it might take a lot longer before they can go through with it."

Choosing a photo with Aunt May holding her baby boy and smiling ever so lovingly, Mika peeled back the plastic that once protected the picture, saying, "I think right and wrong is all perspective anyways. As long as you're happy then that's all that matter."

I challenged her theory asking, "Even if your happiness makes another person miserable?"

With a shrug of a shoulder while cutting the picture down to size, the girl responded, "If you purposely hurt someone just to make yourself happy, then that makes you selfish. Selfish people think they're happy, but they never are."

And with that, the topic was put to rest for the night. Before retiring to my room, I asked Mika why she chose the picture she did. The girl replied, "I think if she was given a second chance, she would have stayed with my dad. So I want to remember grandma as a good mom."

And with Mika planting the picture ever so carefully inside her locket, Aunt May was at last reunited with her family forever and all was forgiven.

Lesson 15: Move On With Purpose

The loss of Aunt May touched all those who knew her. Mika was not the rebellious mess she once was, and the Li's continued going about their household duties but would now always remember the cleaning tips or cooking advice Aunt May left behind. As for myself, I decided that taking one day off a week was not a crime.

For me, the day off was now dedicated to visiting the graves of my parents and Aunt May. In paying respect to them, I was also paying respect to a life that was given to me in which I still had every intention to trudge through. Sometimes, Mika and even Nancy tagged along and I was always grateful of their company.

I began to think of Aunt May's passing not as something that was dark and gloomy; but instead was like a night sky blessed with a full moon and stars surrounding its majestic white light. It was up to us who were still living to find a way that could change a passive night into brightness that embraced the sun's rays. We needed to find that balanced cycle of night and day so that we could find our own solitude.

But today was not my day off. Instead, it was a work day that would see me make the long awaited pitch of convincing my Board of Directors to agree to give our Capersville project a different life.

Aunt May's greatest wish had been for me to find something meaningful. Now, with her gone, I was more determined than ever to see Capersville transform itself into something more than just a money making machine. In a way, this project would commemorate a great woman who once made all the difference in my world and I would stop at nothing until the building was resurrected in her honour. This was now going to be the meaning of my life.

I was first met with skeptical, frustrated looks as I introduced the concept of the new initiative. The Board had already dealt with the Capersville file for many months handling all its obstacles, and to consider having the project take on an entirely new direction was enough to make most of them declare this meeting a waste of time.

But I wouldn't leave without a good fight. I began dissecting all the intricate details of what a new community centre would mean for our company and willed them to see the benefits it would bring for all those involved. And like the skilled business man I had become, I stressed on the financial gains and good will value this new building would bring to our bottom line- even greater than what the original plan was projected to forge. I painted a vision where Capersville would not be like previous files, but instead would be an ongoing project with every intention to be sustainable and profitable for years to come.

When I saw eyes and ears perk at the sight of my new analysis, I knew I had won them over- just as I did with Nancy. For the rest of the pitch, I just needed to entice them a little bit more until they saw only what I saw and nothing else. As the questions started rolling in and I received more and more nods with each confident answer, I knew the entire Board was won over by the new proposal. At the end of the morning, I was given instructions to have a revised proposal and business plan to be reviewed at the end of the month so that construction work could begin within six months.

Before the meeting adjourned, I was challenged with one last question from one of the Board members asking, "Isaac, what will be the name of this new file?"

"Revitalize Capersville," I answered proudly.

After the meeting, I made my way back down to the floor where Nancy and the rest of my team were patiently waiting. All of them had not slept in days as they worked to prepare the presentation I delivered just moments ago. It was beyond words for me to describe the sheer thrill I was experiencing inside. I surprised myself for being able to contain it all as I exited the elevator doors to a group of anxious people looking like they were awaiting a jury's verdict.

Standing in front of the room and trying ever so hard to keep a grin from escaping, I said as solemnly as I could, "Guys….I'm sorry to say we're going to have to throw away the old Capersville file and start drafting a new business plan for Revitalize Capers-…!"

Before I could finish my sentence, a roar erupted as everyone jumped up and down, giving each other hugs and high-fives. Nancy leaned over and gave me a big hug, congratulating all of us for a job well done. For a few minutes, there was nothing but pure joy in the room.

And as quickly as joy came, we all transformed back into mad working bees as Revitalize Capersville began to invade everyone's desks. But nobody seemed to mind the return of chaos and frantic action. Before, when a file was on rush, the work brought only stress and frustration that wore people down until all energy was expelled. But with today's new project, I saw only passion drive my group. It was as though all of them believed that with Revitalize Capersville, their own happiness would be uncovered leading them to nirvana. Perhaps this was the meaning Aunt May had hoped I would find for myself. And though it was a pity I couldn't tell her today that I think I had finally found a purpose in the work that I did, I was comforted to know I was finally at peace. It was a long time coming.

But as I found my own peace, the calm for Mika was broken later that week with an unexpected visitor at home.

Both Henry and Mrs. Li were out running errands and it was my day off. Despite Capersville, I had resisted all temptation to revert back into the workaholic I once was and instructed my team to also give themselves a break. My day off was still used to visit my parents and Aunt May as I had promised I would never forsake them ever again.

Mika was also coming with me that afternoon and as we were about to make our way out, a pounding knock sounded through the door. Reliving a scene from a past both Mika and I wanted to forget, I received a young man drenched with dyed hair of indescribable hues. His attire was even more of a mess, yet it was his eyes that truly chilled my blood the minute I saw him. It was the same venomous glare Mika had used to attack me when we first met. After everything we went through, I had almost forgotten this poison until now.

As I stood in the doorway, drinking in the wreckage that stood before me, I heard Mika gasp as she too saw him. Tightly clenching the door handle, it was as if time had frozen over with nobody saying a word; until finally, Mika asked in a bitter whisper, "Why are you here?"

I cautiously backed away from the door with my fighting instinct intact. He saw my retreat as permission to come inside, though his eyes were kept locked on Mika as he continued to ignore me.

Clearing my throat, I mumbled an excuse to leave the room, but not before making it very clear to Mika that I was nearby if help was needed. Though we were in my territory, I was still worried for Mika's safety.

What felt like an eternity passed until I heard a quiet knock. As it opened, I found Mika calm, yet seemingly anxious at the same time. She entered the room and slumped into a chair as though exhausted from a long fought battle. I gave her time to gather her thoughts, despite feeling my patience quickly running thin. At last the girl spoke.

"He wants money. And I think I need to help him just this once. Can you help me?"

Looking like a puppy asking for love, she raised her eyes at me praying for a miracle. But I felt nothing but pure rage and frustration. I was enraged of her stupidity and frustrated of what she had just asked. I was disgusted that after all that had happened, the girl continued to be duped and fall in the same old trap. She was supposed to be better than this.

"Mika, have you lost your mind? You haven't told me yet, but I bet this loser is Kyle isn't? The same guy who almost cost you your life and now you still want to help him? Are you crazy..?"

"You don't understand, I…"

"You're damn right I don't," I rudely interrupted.

Losing her composure, Mika quickly fired back, "Just be quiet and let me explain."

Soaked with disappointment, I turned my back on the girl with one great huff refusing to look at her. Anger had sealed my lips shut, though my ears were still willing to listen. Seeing my calm temporarily return, Mika began her story, choosing every word with caution.

"You're right, that guy was Kyle. He came here cuz he wants me to repay the money he borrowed for me about a year ago. When we were still together, I saw a diamond bracelet that I really wanted. It's stupid, I know, but every time we walked by the jewelry store I would bug·Kyle to buy it for me. I knew he didn't have the money, so I was really surprised when he gave it to me one day as a gift. About a week later, Noel died. I had the bracelet with me the night of the accident, but I couldn't find it afterwards. He's in trouble now and needs money. I swear, I don't want to have anything to do with him anymore. But I don't want to feel like I owe him anything either. Since I can't find the bracelet, I'm gonna hafta give him the money."

"It's not your responsibility to pay him Mika," I replied. "He chose to give you the bracelet- with or without you nagging him. Technically and legally, you have no obligation."

"You still don't get it, do you?" Mika snapped back, losing her patience. "It's not about the law or responsibility. It's something I need to do to end this all for me so that I can move on. If you don't help me, I'll find another way."

"Is that a threat?" I retorted, offended by her harshness.

I was met with silence before the girl asked flatly once more, "Will you help me or not, Isaac?"

I was about to answer the obvious, when out of the corner of my eye, I saw Aunt May's photo resting comfortably on my book shelf. I was pulled back to a time when she had first proposed the idea of having Mika stay with me, only to face my adamant refusal. An unexpected change of heart led me accepting a strange child into my house and ultimately my life. Despite everything and even now with Aunt May gone, Mika was still here…how quickly time flies. I remembered how this girl nearly lost her life two times over, but was now in front of me, very much alive asking for help.

Her request rested on reasons she figured were right. Though not built on practical sense, she presented an argument based on personal principle. The old Mika who was once a living train wreck would have no doubt stolen the money; yet today's Mika was brave enough to not only approach me, but to also choose to tell me the truth. Did I let my anger come too quickly and get the better part of me?

I took another step closer to the girl who was still holding onto hope and offered a deal.

"I don't care what your reasons are for helping him. But borrowing money has to do with business and law no matter what the original intention is. Do you understand that?"

The girl nodded as I continued. "Good. So, if you get that, then I will lend you the money. But that would mean you now owe me. In exchange for the cash then, I expect you to repay your debt to me through some hard work."

Curious, Mika asked, "What do you want me to do?"

"My company has just sealed a deal on a very important project. And we'll need extra hands to help complete this file. If you take my money, I want you to come and work in the office as an intern for at least 10 hours a week until the project is done. You will do whatever my colleagues need you to do."

"What about school?"

"You decide when you can come into the office, as long as you complete your 10 hours a week. School will still be your first priority, so when you have exams, you need to let me know ahead of time so that alternative arrangements can be made to reshuffle your work in the office. When exams are over, you'll continue coming into the office and deliver on the work you've been assigned. I might not be able to oversee your work all the time, so Nancy will be your main supervisor. Do we have a deal?"

Thinking over my offer, Mika nodded and answered, "Yes."

"Great. How much do you need then?"

"Ten Thousand."

At that, I raised my eyebrows as I reached for my cheque book and said, "Gosh, you kids have such expensive taste, it's ridiculous. I don't want to know where your boyfriend got the money in the first place."

As I handed the cheque over to Mika, the girl reached over taking the money and responded flatly, "Ex-boyfriend...and I don't want to know either."

Shuffling her way out of the study, Mika stopped abruptly in her steps and turned to me once again. As our eyes met, she mumbled, "Thanks for your help, Isaac. I won't let you down again," before leaving me completely alone in the room. She had left too quickly for me to say, "I know you won't."

After Mika handed the money over to Kyle, they parted ways forever and the day moved on as though it were any other weekend. We visited the graves of our loved ones and ended the night with Mrs. Li cooking us a hearty meal.

Except with an announcement to Henry and Mrs. Li that Mika would begin working in my office as an intern beginning next week, not a word was mentioned about the transaction that occurred earlier on.

Later that night, when everyone had retired to their beds, I found Mika sitting out on the balcony in the same place I once found Aunt May. She seemed lost in thought as I took my time approaching her, careful not to startle the girl. Though motionless, Mika looked as though she was staring into a barrel of emptiness- but I knew better than that. I, who had once seen her lay tangled in a bottomless pit, saw a lighted path in front of her now. It warmed my heart to see that the girl had finally found her own peace. This was something her troubled and unfortunate past could not have given before, yet after braving through all the mess, she had come out a survivor and was finally coming home to herself.

No words could describe the transformation I saw in Mika that night. I'm not even sure if she knew it herself but I wanted Mika to rejoice in this new found peace and decided not to disturb her after all. I retired back to my room regretting all the angry words I had ever uttered to her before. The money given to Kyle today was an exchange that gave new life to Mika, and I was grateful to be a part of it. Perhaps through it all, Mika was also helping me find the rest of my peace too.

Lesson 16: Life Choices

Having Mika come work on the new Capersville project was one of the best ideas I ever had. If Kyle never knocked on my door, I would have never thought of this arrangement. Perhaps things really did happen for a reason.

This was the perfect project and perfect time for Mika to come on board and join the team. As Revitalize Capersville was built based on Aunt May's inspiration, it was only fitting to have her grand-daughter also take part in this venture. And as Mika became more and more entrenched in the work, I could see she was also enjoying every minute of it.

At first cautious, not knowing what I had in store for her, Mika was quiet as she soaked in the action that engulfed my team. Once Nancy and I sat her down and briefed her on the details of Capersville, she came to life and jumped at every opportunity to lend a helping hand. She became the eager intern everyone wanted and I couldn't help but feel proud. I silently hoped that Aunt May was also seeing this wherever she was and knew she would be pleased with the woman her grand-daughter was becoming. Aunt May's perseverance, dedication and passion was once again brought back to life through Mika.

I never realized how much Mika resembled her grandmother until now. Her quick wit and humour charmed everyone in the office who worked with her. She proved to be a quick learner and not too long after starting her internship, was invited to sit in on a number of meetings between my company and the city to discuss the partnership that would ultimately recreate Capersville. It didn't take long for everyone to see that this girl had a business savvy about her that impressed even my Board of Directors.

"You better be careful Isaac," one of the Directors teased one day. "Your new intern is quite a catch. I'm gonna have to steal her away from you once she's done school."

"We'll see about that," I challenged as I walked away with a grin on my face like a proud father.

As work on our Capersville file pressed forward, Mika continued to deliver solid performances both in school and at work. Her principal reported that not only had Mika's attendance improved greatly, but that she was also excelling in many of her subjects. With this year being her last year of high school, we were determined to get her into the best college possible. It seemed Mika finally understood that as long as she put in the work, the world would forever be her oyster. It was the most inspirational thing I had ever seen. The girl's transformation was simply amazing as I found myself in disbelief, constantly wondering whether this was still the same person who had landed on my doorstep over a year ago.

Everyday after school, she would have Henry drive her directly to the office and get down to work the minute she tucked her coat and bag away. Despite school exams and assignments, the girl never missed a day of work and only took time off to come with me to visit the graves of my parents and her grandma.

Mika's life was finally on track and equipped with a sense of purpose and I wasn't the only one who noticed. The Li's and Nancy also saw the beautiful butterfly that Mika was slowly morphing into. And when Nancy asked what I did that ignited this change, I could only shrug my shoulders and say it wasn't me at all.

"Mika grow up now," was Mrs. Li's reasoning as Henry nodded alongside his wife adding, "Aunt May must be in heaven to protect Mika and make sure Mika thinking right things."

"Well, you must have done something right," Nancy replied knowingly at me. "People don't change this much over night for no reason. Whatever it was, you should be proud of yourself and for her." I didn't argue with Nancy then. I was in fact very proud of Mika.

That night in the study as I was still gloating over all the recent praise I received about Mika, there was a gentle click that sounded like someone closing a door. Curious, I left the room and headed out into the hallway not knowing what I would find. Following the sound of silent shuffling, it led me once again to the balcony doors where I saw Mika take a seat with a mug in hand, enjoying a midnight breeze.

    Although her back was facing me, Mika's resemblance to Aunt May in her younger years was once again so uncanny I couldn't help but make my way towards her. Hearing someone approach, Mika turned around and was relieved to see that it was only me.

    "Why are you up so late? Did I wake you?" asked Mika settling back in her seat.

    "I wasn't sleeping anyways, and thought maybe you could use some company."

    "Sure, be my guest," she casually replied. Despite all recent life improvements, the girl could still be your typical teenager- raw with attitude and sometimes rude.

    But I accepted her invitation and took a seat next to her unsure of what to say or do next.

    Feigning a cough, I stared out into the dark blanket of nothingness that was in front and asked, "What are you doing up so late?"

    Taking a sip from her mug, Mika shrugged and answered, "Couldn't sleep…some stuff on my mind."

"Are you stressed about school? I know finals are coming up. If you need some time off work, I would be okay with that. You've already put in more than your share of hours these past few weeks. Just let me know…." I offered. I was growing concerned and started to worry that perhaps Mika was feeling too much pressure with everything going on. But those worries were put to rest right away.

"Nah…it's not school or work. I never knew this, but I like being busy. It makes me feel useful and I think I'm doing alright now."

"Well, yeah….you are!" I exclaimed excitedly. "You have any idea how many people have come up to me already to tell me what a great job you've been doing? You should be really proud of yourself Mika. You've come a long way."

"Really?" beamed Mika. "Huh…go figure," she continued in awe, but seemingly happy with what I just told her.

But a mystery still remained.

"So…if it's not school or work…what's on your mind that you can't sleep?" I asked.

Looking at me she hesitated before replying cautiously, "Don't get pissed off, but I was thinking about Kyle."

More curious than angry, I asked, "Why?"

Shrugging her shoulders again, she replied, "Dunno…been just thinking how we met and how things ended between us. Seems like it was a total waste of time- me being with him."

"I wouldn't say it was a complete waste. If it wasn't for him being a complete idiot, I don't think it would have gotten you to be where you are now. I don't know if you've realized this Mika but lots of things have happened since you came to live here and I've learned that things happen for a reason."

"Huh…" pondered Mika. "I guess so…"

"Do you miss him?"

Still cautious of my reaction, Mika replied slowly, "Umm…..sometimes. I know you think he's a total loser- and he is- but there's also something about him that makes me happy; it's like I can't shake this guy off. You know, he used to promise me that he would take care of me and give me a home for us to make a life out of when we got out of school. He said that he would do anything to make me happy. He was the only person who made me feel safe, when nobody wanted me; and I told him stuff I would never tell anyone else. I guess I thought he was the one for me. I mean, when he bought me the bracelet even when he didn't have the money, it made me feel like he would do anything for me. I guess he made me feel like I was worth something."

"Mika, you don't need anyone, let alone a Kyle to make you feel worthy. You have a lot to offer on your own. You know that, don't you?"

She shrugged her shoulders saying, "Sure…I guess. Before grandma, I had nobody. My own mom ditched me and the only person left was dad who never bothered to look at me, let alone love me. But Kyle could have had any girl he wanted, and he chose me because I was special to him."

What a wonder it was for two people who once vowed eternal love to each other only to end a promise as two bitter and spiteful foes. There are some who blame these breaks on character flaws or cheating hearts. But I disagree. To me, matters of the heart always relied on time to determine fault or happiness. It was through the endurance of time that allowed a heart to either fall from grace, harming everyone in its path or to drink up life's passion with a faithful partner where all promises of a happy future would be declared, carrying nothing but pure love.

"I guess that makes you a lucky girl."

"Huh?"

"Even though he turned out to be a let down, at least you know what it feels like to have someone choose to be with you. Some people never even get that chance. So keep on remembering the good things that Kyle was, but don't forgive the bad things he did. When you meet someone else- and I guarantee that you will- make sure the guy not only has the good traits you loved in Kyle, but can also make you a better person. Kyle might have said he cared for you, but if he truly loved you, he would have protected you by making your life better to help you become a better person; and you would have done the same thing for him. That's the only way how two people can survive together."

Seemingly unsure whether to trust or ridicule my advice, Mika decided to be nice anyways saying, "I suppose…but I guess time will tell."

That was the most insightful thing I had heard since knowing the girl. Yes indeed, time will tell all.

But the time now was for us to sleep. As we both got up to head back to our rooms, Mika suddenly stopped and turned to say, "What you just said….there is one thing that I think you're wrong about."

"Really? And what's that?"

"The part where you said that not everyone knows what it feels like having someone choose to be with you. I know you were talking about yourself Isaac, and for the record, you *should* already know what it feels like to have someone choose you."

"I don't understand what you're trying to get at…"

Shaking her head and rolling her eyes in disappointment, she answered impatiently, "Duh…you have Nancy…"

Amused, I shook my head in denial and chuckled with disbelief. "I don't think so. You know that Nancy works for me."

"Really?" challenged Mika. "Then would a person carry a picture of her boss around, unless there was something else going on?"

And with that, the girl quickly dashed off leaving me standing alone dazed and confused.

Lesson 17: Matters Of The Heart

Damn Mika. Her words taunted my mind the entire night, leaving me tossing and turning in bed with no hope of sleep. Was what Mika said true? Did Nancy carry a picture of me around? If it was true, why would she do such a thing?

Then, thoughts of Nancy slowly entered my mind beginning with the first time we met. I had just been promoted into a senior management position and realized I needed an extra set of hands to help with the commotion of appointments, meetings and the handling of chaos from the everyday projects that were bombarding my portfolio.

Nancy had just graduated from college, a business major and eager to show the world what she was made out of. She had an impressive resume and presented well in her interview. I remember being worried that the girl was too young and naïve for the job, but at the same time couldn't help but be impressed of her honesty and enthusiasm out of all the candidates who had applied. While she made it clear this job was intended to be a stepping stone for her career, she also promised that as long as she was in the position she would devote her life to the work. That was about five or six years ago and since being hired, I had not heard Nancy say anything about leaving.

Five or six years. Was it that long already? In a blink of an eye, the small town country girl I had hired to be my assistant had blossomed into a sophisticated woman. It suddenly occurred to me that I too had grown, but in a different way. I had grown to become dependent on Nancy for not only her work in the office, but also as my confidant in life. I recounted all that had happened in the past and realized in my most confused and desperate moments the only time I was able to find solace and direction was after hearing Nancy's advice or seeing her contagious smile.

I wasn't always the ideal boss, and remembered a dark time in my life when all I knew was bitterness and disappointment. There wasn't a doubt in my mind that I must have been less than kind to the people who worked for me, including Nancy. And yet even during those days, Nancy had endured sleepless nights with me in the office time and time again just to meet project deadlines. She gave nothing but her all to produce the perfect product so that I would succeed. When Mika landed in my life, she generously offered herself to help the troubled teen get out of her rut. And when Aunt May was about to leave us, she was by my side ready to cushion my grief.

All that Nancy had done for me I had blindly attributed to the fact that she was just doing her job. While she certainly went above and beyond her duty, I only thought of her as a loyal employee- the best assistant anyone could ask for.

But if what Mika said tonight was true, and that there was something more to Nancy's actions, why had nothing happened yet? Most importantly, why hadn't Nancy said anything to me?

At the same time, another thought dawned on me. Knowing Nancy all this time, I never really once sat down to truly talk with her. Apart from her professional work ethic, I pretty much knew next to nothing about Nancy. I suppose there were moments when I was curious of the kind of person my assistant was, but as quickly as my curiosity came, something else would take priority and the world became all about me once more.

In the dark, I suddenly grew ashamed of the person I had become. Not only had I never voiced my gratitude to Nancy for all she had done for me, I had also neglected her as a person.

But acknowledging all that now would still not solve the mystery. With all my past faults, why would Nancy still keep a picture of me with her? It was no use. The more I thought, the more questions came- questions for which I had no answers to.

I finally scolded myself to sleep and promised that I would ask Mika again of what she had said tonight. As I drifted off, I stopped anymore thoughts from entering my head, allowing only Nancy's gentle smile to once again assure me that all would be well in the morning.

*

Morning finally came as I quickly dressed and swallowed my breakfast before asking Henry to drive both Mika and I together. On any normal day, he would drive Mika to school while I took my own car and everyone would go their separate ways. But today I had questions that only Mika could answer. Though puzzled, Henry nodded when I approached him and got in the car to wait for Mika.

The girl was also surprised when she saw me waiting for her, but got in the vehicle all the same. As the car ride began, I knew it wouldn't take long before we would be arriving at Mika's school. Without wasting anymore time, I asked, "So…what exactly did you mean last night about Nancy keeping a picture of me?" I began, trying to sound as casual as possible, hoping the girl would think nothing of my question.

Toying with a zipper on her school bag, she answered without looking up, "Well, first thing, it's not just a picture of you. It's a picture of both of you. Looks like it was from a party or something."

Still desperately taming my impatience, I pressed on, "Did she tell you about the picture?"

"No…I probably shouldn't have told you about it. I don't think Nancy would want anyone to know…"

"Then…how *did* you know about it?"

"When me and Nancy were working late a few weeks ago, the picture fell out of her bag when we were getting ready to leave the office. When I found it, I wanted to give it back to her, but just never got the chance. Like I said, I shouldn't have told you."

Before I could ask anymore questions, Mika reached inside her bag and handed over a laminated photo. True to Mika's description, it showed both Nancy and I together. Nancy was in a slim, lavender evening gown that had a mini-train flowing gracefully in the back. Her hair was pulled back into a messy bun, but looked elegant as ever. I stood beside her in my evening tux and black shoes. I remember the night the picture was taken. It was at a charity event from a few years ago. I recalled that it was something I had originally decided not to go to, but had my mind changed for me after my boss had strongly encouraged me to attend as it was good publicity for the company. Facing a last minute change in plans and unable to find a suitable partner, I had asked Nancy if she was able to sacrifice a night to go with me. As always, she didn't disappoint and was the perfect partner.

While still staring at the picture and gathering my thoughts, I didn't notice Henry had already arrived in front of Mika's school. I broke from my trance and handed the picture back to Mika.

Shaking her head as she made her way out of the car, Mika mumbled, "No way…it's not my problem anymore. You should give this back to her."

"Me?" I cried in disbelief. "How would I explain why I have this picture?"

Mika shrugged her shoulders and replied, "I dunno…you'll think of something."

"Besides," she added, "that way you can ask her things I can't answer."

"Like what?" I sputtered, embarrassed and bashful.

Rolling her eyes and shaking her head at the same time, Mika answered, "Like why she's keeping a picture of you."

"But…" I protested.

"Ai yo….Mr. Isaac ah, listen to Mika this time…I think she right…keep the picture lah," interrupted a smiling Henry at the front.

Surprised of the unexpected encouragement from my driver, Mika thanked Henry for his support with a smile and shut the car door behind her, leaving me once again baffled and lost.

As the car merged its way back onto the street to join the rest of the morning traffic, questions began to enter my mind again. But who could I ask now? Looking up, I caught Henry still smiling to himself through the rear view mirror. Maybe he knew something I didn't.

"Mr. Isaac, listen to Mika and give picture back to Miss. Nancy," suggested Henry.

"But Henry," I began to protest, "How would I explain how I got the picture?"

"You remember what Mika say? You can think of something. Miss. Nancy also have to explain why she have picture of you too, right? Maybe she get so surprise, you don't have to explain anything."

I still wasn't convinced that it was the right thing to do. And as Henry drove closer and closer to the office, my thoughts became more and more jumbled. I began to wonder just why was I feeling this way? How could a simple picture cause this much agony in such short amount of time?

The car was pulling into the building's parking lot, but I was not ready to go in and face her yet; though Henry felt otherwise. Seeing my hesitation, he turned to me and said, "I think Isaac already know what you need to say, but just scared; I think Miss. Nancy is scared too. That's why she carry picture of you for so long but don't say anything. Isaac should be the man and be brave. Ask what you want to ask and listen to what she say."

"Henry, I don't know how to ask her without making us both feel awkward. I don't want to lose a good assistant over a silly picture, you know?"

"But if Mr. Isaac don't say anything, he might lose good life partner. Before this, you honest and don't know anything. But now, you know what Nancy is thinking and you still don't say anything. Then, now it is you who is not nice."

Looking down at the picture still in my hand, I protested stubbornly, "But who's to say that she kept this picture because of me? What if she's been keeping it for a different reason? Besides Henry, I've never really thought of her as anything more than my assistant. I shouldn't be letting one measly picture change everything."

"Ai-ya...Mr. Isaac!" sighed my driver. "You maybe not think before- but if Miss. Nancy only your assistant, then why you let small picture change your thinking now? Henry have never see you like this before."

"But..."

Holding up his hand stopping anymore stubborn protests and denials, Henry continued to say, "No 'buts' lah...Mr. Isaac just go in and ask. When you see Miss. Nancy you will know what to say and will know what you feel. But don't let lady waiting. Good woman don't wait for you forever."

And with that, Henry coaxed me out of the car and I reluctantly stepped outside like a child refusing to go to school. And as Henry left me still lingering outside the office building, I found myself nervous, anxious, but excited to see Nancy all at the same time; though I still didn't know how I would approach her about the picture.

*

I quickly recovered and gained back composure- at least from the outside- and made my way into the office as though nothing had happened. For the entire morning, while it looked like I was engrossed in work; my mind was doing something else. I had since put the photo in my wallet, and was thinking of the different ways I could return it back to Nancy.

I knew I could secretly just leave the picture in a place where Nancy would easily spot it, and have her quietly retrieve it back with her belongings without anyone knowing. It was a very tempting thing to do and I knew I would be able to go on as though nothing had happened.

But as soon as I began to favour this plan, I heard Henry's voice scolding me for being such a coward. As the day dragged on, I stole quick glances of a busy Nancy and realized that Mika and Henry were right.

Even if I were to pretend that nothing had changed, it wouldn't be true. The fact was, something had already happened and avoiding confrontation would only leave me with more questions. But I didn't know what I was feeling, and for once in a long time didn't know what I wanted. How then, was I to confront her? Nancy deserved answers as much as I did and having me tangled in confusion would not be fair to her either. *Just talk to her Isaac and everything else will work out.*

A choice had to be made; and it was finally decided. I would ask Nancy to lunch and return the photo back to her. I suppose everything else in-between and afterwards would work itself out.

*

Lunch had to be pushed back to dinner, as an unexpected business meeting invaded its way into an already hectic schedule. Before we knew it, mid-afternoon had also passed and soon there was only Nancy and I left in the office. I looked at Nancy who was still working intently and sucked in a breath of air before shoving all fear aside to push myself forward and approach her. But before I could offer a dinner invitation, I heard her voice.

"I'm starving, did you want to grab something to eat with me?"

Taken aback and flustered, I mumbled something that must have resembled a 'yes' because the next thing I knew, Nancy had already shut down her work station and waiting for me to do the same.

I quickly grabbed my things and headed out to the elevators with her. I told Nancy that Henry had driven me to work and asked if she would mind walking to the restaurants nearby. She didn't care where we went as long as there was food. We decided to take the scenic route along the pier and settled on a restaurant with a breathtaking waterfront view.

A memory of a time when Nancy took me to the beach suddenly came to mind and I couldn't help but smile thinking of that special moment. It was just after we had said good-bye to Aunt May and was one of the few times when we did not talk about work schedules, agendas or meetings. I didn't realize it then, but it was because of what she had said that night that I had begun to let a little faith back in my life. Surely, that was something an assistant was not expected to do for her boss.

The waiter brought us our drinks as we continued to soak in the view that was before us, relaxed and relieved to survive another day. With Nancy still admiring our view, I couldn't help but notice how graceful she was. She wasn't a glamorous person, but there was a strength about her that made her addictive. She radiated an aura that was subtle and different from many people. All someone needed to do was to take a little time to be in her presence and he would be intoxicated by an elegance that was unparallel to anything else. It was something I didn't see before until now. She was a beautiful woman inside and out. I decided then that this was the time to bring up what I had been thinking about all day. It was now or never.

Clearing my throat, I let my thoughts guide my words and said, "Nancy, there's something I've been wanting to ask you for awhile."

Turning her attention towards me, she replied, "Yeah...what's that?"

"I remember when we first met and you were interviewing for the job, you said that this was just a stepping stone for your career and that you wanted to eventually open up your own company. Why haven't you started your own PR firm yet?"

A little startled she responded, eyeing me suspiciously, "Are you trying to fire me?"

"Of course not!" I replied quickly. I hadn't even gotten to the real questions and already I was giving out wrong vibes. This was not a good sign. But I was determined to try again.

"No…" I repeated. "I was just thinking the other day that it's been what- five or six years since you've started working for me…"

"Actually, seven…" interrupted my assistant.

"Seven? Has it been that long already?"

With a smile, Nancy replied knowingly, "Yep…"

"Wow… now I really do feel like an ass…"

"Don't worry, you've been busy."

"Still…that's not an excuse. But that's exactly what I've been wondering about. After all this time, you're still working for me. I know I haven't been a really good boss to you- horrible in fact at times, and you've still toughed it out with me…how come?"

Taking a sip from her glass before responding with a smile, "It really hasn't been all that bad, Isaac. And you haven't been as terrible as you say you've been. Besides, when I first worked for you, I was fresh out of school. It was good for me to have a tough boss like you. It helped build character and a thicker skin."

"But what about your original plans of starting your own company?"

"I still think about it sometimes, but somehow, it's just not the right time. I like the work I do now and I know I do a good job for you and the office…"

"Even if you have to put up with a crabby old boss?" I teased.

"Well...yeah. I have to admit, you were a little difficult to please at first, but nothing I couldn't handle. And lately, I don't know if you've noticed, but you've changed, Isaac. There's a softer side to you now, and I think that's a good thing."

Curious, I asked, "What do you mean?"

"Don't take this the wrong way, but the old Isaac I knew before was sad and miserable all the time and he took it out on people at work. It seemed like you thought the whole world owed you something. But I've noticed that ever since Mika popped into your life, you've become happier. You might not have realized this, but the people around you have all seen you change, Isaac. It's a good thing though. There must have been something in your life that was missing before, but I think you've found it now."

"So, why did you put up with my crap? You really only had to work for me a few years and leave to do what you really wanted."

"I know...but there was something about you that made me want to stay. I think it was because of your ridiculously high demands that motivated me to do more at work. In your own way, you're actually a really good teacher. I've learned a lot from you."

Flattered of her compliment, I smiled, relishing in the moment.

Without thinking, I reached for my wallet and pulled out the photo that had nagged my conscience the entire day. Nancy saw the picture and realized it was hers.

Suddenly shy and no longer her confident self, she took the picture from my hand and asked without making eye contact, "How did you get this?"

Cautiously choosing my words, I answered, "It was actually Mika who told me you had dropped this. But things have been so busy she didn't get a chance to give it back; so she passed it onto me to return to you since we see each other more often."

"But…Mika's been in the office everyday up until today…"

"Well…you know kids…always so absent minded," I scrambled quickly. "That's probably why she gave me the picture instead since she knows she'll keep on forgetting to give it back to you."

Unsure whether she believed my fib, she responded slowly with, "Ok…"

Not wanting to give her anymore time to think about what I had just fabricated, I asked, "Nancy…can I ask you why you've kept the picture with you all this time? I remember this was taken a few years ago already."

"Umm…." Nancy began, as though searching for the right words herself. It was as though she knew she was trapped with nothing to do but to expose the secret she once thought safe from the world. There was something endearing seeing her flustered and embarrassed for once.

Passing the picture back and forth between her fingers and glancing timidly at me, she replied, "This was the only picture I had of just us two together and I wanted to keep it."

At her response, my mind turned blank as I grew speechless not knowing how to continue the conversation. This was one of the few times in my life where I had no idea- absolutely nothing. I was ashamed of my ignorance and shocked that an amazing person like Nancy would choose me.

But the silence grew unbearable for us both and Nancy decided to take the next step, despite how vulnerable she must have felt after what was just said. "Listen Isaac," she stressed, "I never planned on saying or doing anything. I was happy enough keeping this picture and nothing else. I admit there have been times when I've imagined what it would be like if we were more than just co-workers or friends, but I have never,

ever let it interfere with my work. I hope this doesn't give you a reason to change things between us….work-wise."

"Nancy, you're nothing but exceptional around the office all the time. But to be honest, I'm shocked. From the moment Mika gave me this, I have been confused and don't know really what to think."

"Then don't think about anything and pretend nothing happened," offered Nancy.

I shook my head reasoning, "I have to admit, I did think about doing that. It would have been really easy just secretly leaving the picture somewhere for you and pretend nothing happened. But I couldn't do it Nancy. I guess I needed to know what exactly you've been thinking about all this time."

"So now you know. What happens next?" asked Nancy flatly.

"Well…." I began slowly as I waited for my thoughts to form, "What would you say if I were to suggest we try being together- not together as boss and employee, but together as a couple?"

Without a second thought, Nancy asked, "Why?"

I fumbled and managed to stutter out a clumsy answer with, "B-b-because…it's the next natural step for us after what you just told me isn't?"

Irritated and even annoyed, Nancy asked, "Isaac, do you blindly date anybody who says they have an interest in you?"

"Well…I haven't dated many people, but the women I have gone out with before have been pretty direct with what they wanted."

"That's not answering the question," Nancy challenged.

"I don't know what you're trying to get at Nancy," I shot back feeling my own impatience. What did this girl want? I had generously offered giving each other a chance, but instead of acceptance, I was being attacked.

"Ok, then let me ask you a basic question. Before tonight, have you ever thought of me- thought of us- as more than just friends?"

"To be honest, no, I haven't," I answered.

"If this picture didn't suddenly pop up, would you have ever thought about me romantically?"

"No…probably not ever…No! I didn't mean it that way!" I exclaimed, but I knew it was too late. I had been tricked and the damage was already done with my chance with Nancy slowly but surely slipping away.

"That's what I'm trying to get at Isaac," said Nancy. "I won't be with someone who decides to be with me only because of obligation or guilt, or that he wants to be nice. This isn't how these things work.

"Nancy, you've got it all wrong. I didn't mean to say that I would have *never* considered us together. It's just that things have been so hectic for me lately and you've been such a natural part of my life, the thought just never came up. But if later down the road…who knows…," and before I could stop the rest of my words from escaping, I knew it was no use. I had once again unintentionally downgraded Nancy's importance.

But Nancy was no longer angry or annoyed. Instead, I saw a return of her familiar smile as she reached over and calmly patted my hand telling me not to panic.

"It's alright Isaac," she began. "You don't have to do this. Actually, for you to even attempt to do what you just did shows that you're not a bad person. But I'm also not willing to settle. What I feel towards you, is just me. I'm not some business deal that you need to consider by weighing the pros and cons. You don't have a responsibility and you're definitely not obligated to do anything for me."

"But Nancy…" I tried again, only to be cut off.

"You're not ready for me, Isaac."

"But I think I might be," I argued.

"No, you're not," replied Nancy firmly. "For you to panic like this even before anything has even happened tells me you're still unsure. And quite frankly, I don't want to be with someone who isn't in love with me no matter how much I'm into him. Do you understand what I'm saying, Isaac?"

Oh gosh, did she just say love?

"But what if I was willing to try? I admit, I don't know if I'm in love now…but I'm willing to try and take the time to find out."

"But I'm not willing to be your experiment to see whether you think we can be together or not."

"You're twisting my words. I didn't mean it that way-"

And before I tried to redeem myself once more, Nancy heaved a sigh and said, "I think we should sleep on this Isaac. If you're really serious about giving us a chance, then entertaining the idea at a later time shouldn't change anything right?"

Not being one to force someone into anything that didn't feel right, I relented and checked one last time saying, "If that's what you truly want, then I'll wait."

Satisfied, Nancy looked back at me and said, "It is. And in the meantime, promise me that things will stay the same at work?"

I looked back at my assistant and replied, "Absolutely."

Lesson 18: Second Chances

To my surprise, the rest of the night went well. I didn't realize how famished both of us were until our food came and we swallowed it down like a pack of hungry wolves. In between bites, I found out a lot more about Nancy- things I probably should have known and asked about years ago when she and I first met. I learned that she grew up in a small town about two hours or so away from the city. An only child to working class parents, she paid her own way through college by working two to three jobs while studying.

She shared with me some of the hardships she had to endure as a child. Her father had always wanted a son- not a daughter and after years of trying for a second child but to no avail, her father simply withdrew away from his family of women. Her memory of him was of an unhappy soul. Though he never physically harmed them, he took his anger out on his wife and daughter using verbal attacks and demeaning insults.

"But my mom was a really strong woman," explained Nancy. "I remember trying to convince her to divorce my dad, but she always said he would still be my dad no matter what. Divorcing him wouldn't change that, and it wouldn't change the fact we would still always be family."

Living under the cloud of being an unwanted child, Nancy forced herself to make a choice. She chose to ignore her father's insults and focused on education. To her, that was the gateway to freedom for both her and her mother.

Years later, Nancy finally succeeded and her mother proudly saw her daughter pave a better life for herself. Eventually, Nancy's mother did file for divorce and moved into her own place to start a new life. After the separation, Nancy's father refused to have anything to do with either of them and since then neither Nancy nor her mother had heard from him.

"Why would you still want to know how he is even after all he did to you and your mom?" I asked in disbelief.

Pausing in thought, Nancy replied, "I think I would be curious to see how he is, just because he's my dad. But I'm not angry with him anymore. I mean, looking back, I guess he could have been a lot worse. He never was physically abusive and I didn't ever see him touch a drink. He was just a really unhappy guy and couldn't see the good in anything. Besides, seeing how great my mom is now and that my life turned out alright, I guess I wish for his sake that he's doing okay too."

"That's pretty big of you for thinking that way," I said in admiration.

Shrugging her shoulders, Nancy said, "It takes a lot of energy being angry at someone. The way I see it, your life is dealt with a certain set of cards and you just have to work with that set the best you can. You can't control people- even if they are your family. The only thing you can do is choose whether you want to be happy or not for yourself. You really can't blame anyone for your own misery."

"Wow Nancy…I had no idea…"

"It's no big deal. Millions of people suffer more crap than what I've been through. My life could have been a lot worse. At least I have a great mom that takes the place of a father I never had, right?"

"I suppose," I replied, still not fully convinced that she should be satisfied with her life just like that.

Her one story turned me into a small petty person. The bitterness and resentment I had felt in my world mattered so very little. While I faulted my parents for never accomplishing anything great in their lives, at least they had given me care, protection and a complete home. They gave me Aunt May to take care of me after their leaving and through an indirect way was my inspiration to achieve success in life. And yet, for the longest time, I chose to be unhappy and blamed everyone for my misery- and for what purpose?

Our conversation moved on as we began to talk about past relationships. Nancy told me about old boyfriends who had broken her heart and about other boys whom she had rejected. In turn, I shared stories of old girlfriends- all whom I met after the world began to think I had struck success. I felt safe telling her the ridiculously expensive things these women would make me buy only to realize in the end they were not in love with me, but with my bank account.

"Ha…I could have told you that," teased Nancy who was clearly entertained by these stories of mine.

"So...have you ever gone after a girl?" asked Nancy.

"To be honest…never. I never went out with anyone when I was in school and the few girls I dated afterwards all came after me first. It's still a mystery why I ended up going out with them in the first place. I guess maybe it was some kind of infatuation of wanting to know what it was like to be with someone exclusively. I have to admit, it did feel good initially; but after awhile, it just seemed like I was always dating the same type of superficial, shallow people. I got fed up and gave up on this whole relationships thing. There isn't much point to it anyways."

"Well, to be fair," reasoned Nancy, "You didn't make the smartest choices with the company you kept and have no one to blame but yourself."

Smiling, I answered, "Yeah…I suppose you're right…as always."

The rest of the evening continued with casual, relaxed dialogue without any pressure, expectations or passing of judgment. I opened myself up to her like I had never done before with anyone else. We were simply two people getting to know each other, appreciating each other's life experiences and accepting the mistakes we had made in our past lives.

At the end of dinner, Nancy offered to drive me home and I accepted. The car ride was done mostly in silence, but it was a silence that was stripped from any awkward quiet that would have made for an uncomfortable journey. Simply having Nancy by my side was enough to make me content. I wondered if Nancy felt the same way.

Pulling up to my building, I thanked Nancy for the ride and wished her a safe drive home. Before getting out of the car, I turned to Nancy and with hopeful eyes said, "I had a really great time tonight and hope we can do this again."

With a smile Nancy replied back, "We'll see."

I couldn't keep my heart-felt grin from escaping onto my face. It was the most real, honest happiness I had ever experienced.

*

I returned home to see Henry and Mrs. Li sitting eagerly on the couch. They were like parents waiting anxiously for their son to come home from his prom date. Seeing Mrs. Li's hopeful smile, I knew Henry must have told her about this morning's conversation.

Sure enough, as soon as I hung up my jacket and tucked away my work bag, they couldn't contain themselves any longer and the questions began. Did I ask Nancy about the picture? How did I ask her about the picture? Did I tell Nancy how I felt about her? How did I felt about her? Were we together now? Offering answers left and right, I was not allowed to spare any details.

I told them about dinner with Nancy and of her reaction when I showed her the photo. To their disappointment, I then went onto describing how the girl tactfully rejected my offer to be together, despite all efforts.

"Ai-yo...," moaned Mrs. Li shaking her head. "You don't ask girl like that. She is not business. You have to be more caring...more like gentleman mah!"

Chuckling alongside his wife, Henry glanced in my direction and asked, "But you look happy. Nancy say 'okay' in the end?"

I smiled and shook my head saying, "No...she was pretty adamant to not have me rush into things with her. So we're still the same...I'm her boss and she's my assistant. But we did have a really good time talking and getting to know each other tonight."

"And....?" pushed Mrs. Li. She was like a love-struck teenager wishing for a happy ending for her favourite characters.

"And... I learned lots of things about Nancy I didn't know before. I don't know exactly how to explain this but she's different than the girls I'm used to, and definitely someone who knows what she wants and not willing to settle for anything less."

"Ah...," nodded Henry with approval. "That is because Miss. Nancy is strong lady and she have respect."

"Yah, Yah!" chimed in Mrs. Li. "She is not...what you call it? Something digging...?"

"You mean she's not a gold-digger?" I offered, completing her thoughts.

"Yes!" exclaimed my excited housekeeper. "She is not go-diggah."

Patting my shoulder, Henry said, "Miss. Nancy is good girl. Do you like her more than assistant?"

"To be honest, I think I always took Nancy for granted...probably because she's always been there for me. But now... I think of her differently."

Henry replied smiling, "Then you take more time to make Miss. Nancy see. I think Miss. Nancy want to hear what you just say to Henry. And she probably want to know what you feel, not think."

"Isaac, always think too much," added Mrs. Li. "That's what Aunt May always say."

And in remembrance of Aunt May, I promised both Henry and Mrs. Li that I would work hard to win Nancy's heart. But in the meantime, asked if they would release me for the night so that I could rest. A lot had happened today, and I was beginning to feel fatigue take over my bones.

We said good night and as I turned the corner, I noticed Mika's vacant room. Curious where she was, I asked Mrs. Li and she replied with a smile that she was out with a boy called Steve.

Surprised that Mika and the boy were still in touch, I paused for a moment trying to recall what my last encounter with Steve was like. Mrs. Li reassured me saying, "No worry…this one is good for Mika."

Comforted that Mika's date was approved by my trusty housekeeper, I nodded with a smile and retired to my room for the night.

But no matter how tired I was, sleep ignored me and refused to come. For the second night in a row, Nancy took over my mind. Ideas of how to make Nancy believe that I truly wanted to be with her circled around in my head over and over again. I wanted her to know that it wasn't because of obligation or pity, but that for once in my life, I felt happiness that could only be felt when I was with her.

And as I replayed what had happened at dinner, I realized that while I was rejected tonight, Nancy had in fact given me another chance. I had to make her believe that even though I may have been slow to react, she had indeed become something so substantial in my life that I now knew I needed her to be a permanent pillar by my side.

Then from Nancy, my thoughts wandered over to Mika who was still not home. While it was good to see her gain back a social life, I couldn't help but worry whether she would once again fall into something she would regret later on. I believe she had learned a valuable lesson from Kyle, but also knew people had short memories and forgot all too quickly. I was afraid Mika would once again forget to think with her head and act on girlish infatuation, foolishly mistaking it for love.

As I continued to wonder whether Mika would be strong enough this time to distinguish between right and wrong, a door opened and closed followed by muffled footsteps in the distance. Since I couldn't sleep anyways, I got up and made my way out into the hallway hoping to bump into Mika before she retreated back to her room.

But her room was still empty, and as I was deciding whether it was my imagination or had I in fact really did hear the door, I detected movement in the kitchen. Following the noise, I found Mika fixing herself a cup of tea.

I feigned a cough as I entered the kitchen. Mika looked up and smiled offering me some tea too. I accepted and took a seat at the kitchen table with her.

"So…how did your day go?" asked Mika slyly.

Like a broken record, I recounted the events that happened with Nancy just as I did earlier with Henry and Mrs. Li. She listened the entire time except for an occasional chuckle when I described instances of my verbal clumsiness that must have made me look like a ridiculous fool. And at the end of my story, I shared with Mika my dilemma of how to win the heart of someone as special as Nancy.

Shaking her head, Mika answered, "I wouldn't know. You're on your own with this one."

"What?" I exclaimed. "You were the one who started this whole thing in the first place and now you're ditching me?"

Smiling as though taunting me, she replied, "Hey…I was doing both of you a favour. One was too scared to do anything and the other was too blind to see. It was because of me that you guys were able to be honest with each other. And besides, it sounds like she's willing to give you a second chance which means you haven't lost her yet. This part's easy. Just do some prince-charming act and you'll win her over."

I rolled my eyes saying, "If only it was that easy. We're talking about Nancy here remember…she's smart and won't fall for that kind of thing."

Nodding her head knowingly Mika replied, "That's true…lucky for you, Nancy's got a brain. I dunno…just keep on being the way you've always been and find another time to sit down and convince her you're serious and not playing around. I think the main thing is to not treat her any differently, and remember to just be you. That was what attracted her to you in the first place."

While it seemed surreal taking advice from her, I appreciated the girl's wisdom and nodded my head saying, "You're right. I guess I just have to remember to be patient so that she doesn't think I'm rushing into things. Makes sense…"

Taking a sip from her cup, Mika asked casually, "So I'm assuming Mrs. Li told you about Steve? I'm guessing that's why you're still not sleeping yet in the first place?"

Without defending myself I answered, "I was just a little surprised, that's all. I didn't know you still kept in touch with him."

Taking another gulp of tea, Mika replied, "Steve has always been a great friend."

"Is he just a friend or something else now that Kyle's out of the picture?" I asked directly.

"Hmmm….I don't know yet," answered Mika honestly. "Maybe that was one of the reasons I went out with him today. I know he's a really good guy and all, but I was so busy with Kyle and everything else before, I never took the time to think about him differently. Kinda like how you were with Nancy."

I nodded, fully appreciating what she meant.

"So I guess you could say tonight was the first time we went out on an official date. But I think I still need some time. Besides, I'm not in a rush to do anything stupid again. I figured if Steve has been waiting for me all this time, then what's a little while longer."

"Poor Steve…" I said with a smile. "But I think you're doing the right thing Mika. You're both young and have all the time in the world. And you're right about Steve too. I'm hardly an expert on these things, but as a guy, if he truly was for real and into a girl, he would be willing to wait for her."

"Yeah…that's what I figure too," agreed Mika.

My night ended for the second time as Mika and I parted ways down the hall. I took cover under my blankets once more hoping my luck with sleep would improve this time round. As I laid in bed, I gradually felt my eyelids grow heavier and heavier. As the world around me blurred away into darkness, I found myself thinking of Aunt May again. Today was the first time in a long time both Mika and I had given ourselves a second chance to know love again. Aunt May would have been pleased.

Lesson 19: Cherish Your Time

Time is a very unique substance. There are moments when it can be slower than a tortoise sunbathing on a beach, and just when you're certain it has lost all its ability to move, it strikes forth faster than the speed of light.

That's what happened to me. One minute I had abruptly come to a complete stop still so confused of what my next steps should be and the next minute, found Revitalize Capersville in its final stages of completion.

As with many things, money and politics invaded our Capersville project. Someone realized that a city election was looming ahead and the mayor became obsessed to have the Capersville building completed before ballots were cast. He was running for re-election and hoped that voters would see all the good he was doing for his people. As an incentive, more money than what we expected was granted to fund construction on the condition that the project be fast tracked. Taking up the opportunity, we quickly launched what was once a three year plan into an aggressive 18- month project.

Time soon became an even more valuable commodity. We made use of every minute out of every day working on the building construction. It was as though everyone in the office including Mika became obsessed; convinced that Capersville would be the signature piece that marked the significance of our livelihood. And in a way I think it was. There wasn't anything else that had the same meaning or purpose as Capersville. From the moment it was decided that the building would be given new life, this was going to be *the project* everyone would reminisce and tell their grandkids about, years to come. In a way, we were working for our future.

And as we all devoted our lives to work, I remembered Mika's advice and stayed true to my word. Life went on just as before. I continued to be Nancy's boss while she worked just as diligently being my reliable assistant. Nobody would have guessed that something beyond work had happened between the two of us months ago.

But while we feigned normality on the surface, things had indeed changed- at least for me. I had grown to be more attentive to Nancy and was beginning to mould a different me in the course of it all. I got better controlling my temper and learned to appreciate that patience was indeed a great virtue. I uncovered the importance of humour in the office and became pleasantly surprised to discover I had in fact, a team of very competent people working for me.

And while I grew to enjoy more of people's company, Nancy had become the main priority in my life and I wanted to make sure she was protected. When work called for us to stay late into the night, I offered to drive her home concerned of her safety. If there were days she was suffering a cold or flu, I insisted she take time off to recover. At work, if I felt she was taking on too much, I suggested she share the workload with the rest of our colleagues.

There were days when she accepted my offers of good will and there were other times I was gently declined. Whether I agreed with her or not, I always respected her choices and never pushed for more than what she wanted or felt comfortable with. I was beginning to see that perhaps this was what Nancy had wanted for me to realize. Two people relating to each other should be this harmonious, without any pressure or force. There should be no discomfort or embarrassment, only genuine concern for the one you care for. At the end of the day, whether we were together or not, seeing her smile and happy was enough for me.

Another new found joy of mine was Mika. After much thought to her future, she finally decided to enroll in Business School. I suspect the Capersville project had made her realize just how much she enjoyed the excitement and pressure of the business world. Mika had proved herself over and over again what a vital asset she was to us all in the office and was offered a permanent position with the organization. And so, it was decided that when Mika started taking up higher education, she would also continue her internship. I couldn't have asked for more.

This night, we found ourselves working late once again on Capersville. The file was nearing completion and Nancy and Mika were helping me prepare documents for a meeting with city officials for the next morning. Pleased the work was finally done for the day, I suggested that the three of us go out for a late dinner. Though exhausted, we were also starving and soon found ourselves in a restaurant devouring the food we had ordered.

After savaging down a few bites and with her mouth still full, Mika asked, "So how close are we with finishing the Capersville project? From the outside, it looks like it's already done."

Reaching for my water to wash down my food, I replied smiling, "We're really, really close. Just a few more finishing touches is what I was told today. In fact, one of the things we're talking about tomorrow is setting a date for our grand opening."

Nodding her head excitedly, Nancy chimed in, "I can't believe that we actually pulled it off. I mean, when we were told to cut the time line by literally half, I honestly didn't think it was possible."

Agreeing with Nancy, Mika laughed, "No kidding…kudos to Isaac for leading the way!" And with that, she raised her glass in a toast.

Flattered, I playfully clinked Mika's glass and said, "We'll do a formal toast when it's completely done. But it wasn't all me. Everyone slaved really hard this past year and a half. But hopefully it'll be worth it."

"It will be," said Nancy decisively.

And as dessert arrived, Mika asked, "I know we were putting this off till the end, but does the building have an official name yet? We can't keep calling it Revitalize Capersville forever."

I shook my head and answered, "No…not yet. That's another thing we need to discuss with everyone involved."

"Do you have any thoughts on it?" asked Nancy.

"Not a name exactly…"

And now, looking directly at Mika, I continued to say, "But I was thinking of naming it after Aunt May. She was the inspiration that started this project after all."

Beaming happily, Mika clapped her hands in excitement like a little girl on Christmas morning exclaiming, "I think that's an awesome idea! Can I think of a few names and throw them your way?"

Chuckling I replied, "Of course you can."

Our night continued on with Mika venting about the pressures of school. We then fantasized about our ideal vacation spots while both Nancy and Mika joked that everyone should be given a year's paid holiday with all the work that had been done by the team.

The good humour and company ended all too quickly and soon we had to call it a night as Henry pulled up alongside the restaurant's entrance ready to drive us back home.

We all filed into the back of the car like obedient school children. Henry, seeing us all in good spirits smiled through his rear view mirror and said, "Everyone have good night?"

Nodding, I answered on behalf of our entourage with, "It's been a fantastic night Henry. Capersville is almost done and I'm here with the two most beautiful ladies on a dinner date. What more can a man ask for?"

Nancy playfully punched my shoulder as Henry chuckled saying, "You right Mr. Isaac. You very lucky have two pretty girls. Henry only have one Mrs. Li and she already old…ai-ya… don't tell her I say that. I always tell her she still young."

"Oh Henry…" teased Nancy. "Mrs. Li *is* young compared to you isn't she?"

"Haha…," laughed Henry. "Miss. Nancy right. My woman always be young and pretty when she beside me. That's why I say she can't go anywhere, because I am only man for her that make her look good. When she hear that, she say she is stuck with me always now."

As Henry beamed with pride and adoration over his wife, we couldn't help but feel giddy all over again. To find someone in this complicated world of ours who you can depend on for loyalty and trust was already a difficult thing to do. But to find a soul mate willing to be with you, through the good and bad asking nothing in return except for love was rare and near impossible. How I envied Henry and Mrs. Li and desired the life they led together as one. I wished with all my heart I would also one day find someone who would want to accompany me for the remainder of my days.

Also touched by the man's love for his life partner, Nancy reached over and patted Henry's shoulder saying, "Henry, I think you and Mrs. Li should be very proud for having such a successful marriage together."

Flattered, Henry replied smiling, "No lah…we fight very much…you just don't see. But you want to know secret to happy marriage and long life? I hear long time ago and think it is very right."

Striking our curiosity, Mika asked, "What's the secret?" on our behalf.

With a mischievous smile, Henry answered, "People say 'happy wife, happy life'. I think it is very true. Mrs. Li think so too. So now, when we fight I let Mrs. Li win no matter what because Henry want to live a long life."

Amused of Henry's new found life motto, we laughed and couldn't help but to agree. If anything, it certainly pleased the women who were in the car with us at that moment.

Mika suddenly turned to me as we approached a stop light and said, "Hey...we're near the Capersville work site now. Can we drive by and see what it looks like at night?"

I couldn't deny the girl's hopeful eyes and asked Henry to make a few extra turns towards our beloved building. Little did we know, I was in fact leading us into catastrophe.

*

People who have lived and survived through trauma often describe how time seems to freeze and go into slow motion through the chaos. I can attest and confirm that in a moment of disaster, time does indeed stop.

My memory will only let me remember three things: screeching tires, being tossed violently to one side and then darkness. After that, there were faint echoes of indistinct yelling that blurred in and out of my consciousness. I was spared from feeling any bodily sensation until I opened my eyes to Nancy's voice gently coaxing me back to life.

It felt as though I had been asleep for a hundred years and that I had not used my limbs for even longer a time until now. I saw right away that my arms were hooked to an IV tube and my left leg was wrapped in what looked like a cast though it wasn't elevated. My cheekbones felt as though they had been shattered into a million pieces before being glued carelessly back together again and my head seemed like it was preparing itself for an explosion. What had happened and where was I now?

I reached deep into my memory bank as far back as my throbbing head would allow. I recounted dinner with Nancy and Mika; and lots of laughing as Henry picked us up from the restaurant. There was more laughter as Henry shared with us his secret for a long and happy marriage. I remember someone had wanted to go somewhere other than home and after that….nothing.

I willed my eyes to refocus and saw Nancy rise from her chair as I slowly came to. While reaching for the button to call the nurse, she leaned forward and asked with a gentle whisper of concern, "How are you feeling?"

I winced in pain as I strained a cough to clear a dry throat and struggled up into a sitting position with Nancy's help. I saw she had a tensor wrapped around her wrist and a massive purple bruise on her forehead, but other than that, was still the beautiful woman I remembered her to be.

Ignoring her question, I asked, "What happened?"

"We were in a car accident, Isaac. Do you remember anything at all?" she said softly.

Once again, I searched my memory wanting to go back in time so that I could remember what had happened. Again, I could only go as far back as sitting in the car with Henry driving us to some place. And then…nothing once more.

I recounted all that I could remember to Nancy and waited for her to complete the history as she tightly clutched my hand.

"We were going to go home, but then decided to drive by the Capersville building. While we were going there, a truck ran through a red light and crashed into us. The police confirmed it was a DUI."

Nancy paused as I nodded. Hearing her words, I was finally beginning to remember. The laughter, Mika's excitement as she asked to see the Capersville Building and the sudden jolt of a world being hurled into a black hole was all coming back to me. But I still did not know what had happened afterwards and asked Nancy to continue on. With her eyes never leaving me, she took a deep breath and continued saying carefully, "Isaac, two people died in the crash. The truck driver who ran the light died on impact and…."

…And…? Why was Nancy stopping? Was she summing up the courage to tell me that we had lost Mika? While I needed to know what Nancy had to say, another part of me was silently begging her not to speak. As long as I didn't know, my world would still be intact. But that would not happen as Nancy choked back tears forcing herself to tell the ending of a tragic mishap.

Overcome by sadness, Nancy sobbed, "Isaac, when the truck was coming towards us, Henry already saw it coming and on impulse, he swerved the car in front of the truck so that it would hit his side. They told me that if Henry didn't do that, we would all have been in a lot worse shape than now."

Heaving a heavy sigh and bracing myself for what was to come next, I asked flatly, "What happened to Henry?"

Lowering her head, Nancy answered softly, "We were all rushed to the ER. Henry had severe head injuries, broken limbs and massive internal bleeding. It was just too much for him…"

And just like that, I was told that my most loyal, trustworthy chauffeur, mentor, friend and saviour had his time taken away from him… just like that.

Lesson 20: Love Lost, Love Found

At a time when I should have felt denial, grief, pain, or even anger, I felt nothing. My heart simply closed down, shutting out all emotion. It was a numbness that took over my body and my thoughts, as whatever little hope I had before was ripped away the second Henry was taken. I cursed anyone who had ever led me to believe that the world was filled with prospect and promise because they were all liars. Hope and faith were nothing but cruel creatures that thrived on watching people lose in their game of hide and seek. I had been tricked over and over again, but would not play with them anymore. It was better to be nothing from now on. There was no purpose for existence when life was this fragile and could be disintegrated in an instant. I begged my mind to stop thinking so that I could go on feeling empty.

But instead, it reminded me about the first time Henry and I met. I remembered the diligent worker Henry was and how he would tell me in his own special way that everything always worked itself out, no matter how hopeless. And I remember what a wonderful husband he was to Mrs. Li.

At the thought of Henry's wife, I forced my mind to leave the past and with a heavy heart confronted reality. It dawned on me that there was someone else that had suffered an even greater loss than all of us combined. The least I could do was brave this tragic end on our behalf in hopes of shielding some of the pain Henry's widow was surely enduring now.

"Isaac...are you feeling alright?" asked a worried Nancy.

Forcing a weak smile in hopes of relieving her concern, I answered, "I'm fine. How are you doing? And how's Mika and Mrs. Li now?"

"I'm alright...just scratched up a bit with a sprained wrist. Thank goodness Mika was sandwiched between the two of us so she was protected enough to get away with a few bumps and bruises, but nothing serious. I think she's with Mrs. Li in the cafeteria now. All three of us have been here with you since last night after the accident."

Right at that moment, Mika and Mrs. Li entered the room along with a doctor and nurse. My vitals were checked and I learned I had suffered a concussion which explained the massive headache and had a broken leg. Other than a few other obvious minor injuries, I was a lucky bastard who escaped something that could have been far worse and would recover just fine. But I knew it wasn't luck that saved me. It was Henry and now he was gone.

Finishing what he needed to do, the doctor exited the room but not before reminding us to rest so that we could all regain our strength. Once he was gone, I turned to Mrs. Li who had tears glistening in her eyes.

I reached for her as she leaned forward to hold my hand, and before I could offer any words of sorrow, she was already saying to all of us, "Everyone no say 'sorry'. Henry is good man to everyone and he leave like a hero…he is my hero. Mrs. Li not sad but proud…so Isaac and everyone should also be the same or else will make Henry sad…you know?"

Whatever angry self-pity I had felt moments ago was put to shame with Mrs. Li's words. The minute Henry sacrificed his life, I was obligated to live on despite all hardships. I had no right to give up on life now as I would be forever in Henry's debt.

There was no need then to offer anymore words of comfort. Those words would only carry weight if we lived well- and that was something only time could tell. Bravely wiping away the remains of her tear drops, Mrs. Li announced she needed to go home to begin preparing for Henry's service. She wanted it to be held as quickly as possible so that Henry's strong spirit would not be left out in the cold.

Nancy who was just discharged from the hospital, offered to take a cab home with Mrs. Li. Without words, I looked at Nancy as she gathered her belongings, and thanked her silently. As she smiled back at me, I knew she understood what I wanted to say. Before leaving, Nancy promised to come back early the next morning leaving only Mika and I in solemn silence.

It looked as though Mika had aged ten years over night. Her shoulders carried a burden that a girl her age should not have been carrying; and her eyes held a sorrow that would drive the strongest soul down to his knees in tears. I knew that unless I could turn back time, there was nothing I could do that would make her misery disappear. Perhaps grief is a necessary evil to help a person truly appreciate happiness when it does finally come.

Dropping her head in hopeless shame, Mika mumbled, "I should have just let Henry drive us home. If I didn't open my stupid mouth, none of this would have happened. This was all my fault. I killed Henry."

"Hey...," I replied sternly as I pulled myself as upright as my body would possibly allow. "You listen closely to me Mika- none of this, and I mean nothing that happened was your fault at all. If there needs to be blame, then blame the idiot drunk who did this to us and from what I heard, he's gone now too; so as far as I'm concerned, justice has been done."

Mika raised her head to meet mine- her eyes were stained a bloodshot red from a night of crying. I saw that she still wasn't convinced and continued saying, "What about me then? I was the one who told Henry to take the shortcut turns. If it wasn't for my directions, he wouldn't have slammed himself into the truck."

Met with a sobbing girl's silence and remembering a lesson I had learned about choices, I continued on saying, "Mika, we can spend our whole life passing blame back and forth, but it won't bring Henry back. Did you see how brave Mrs. Li was just now? You and I know she must be devastated losing the love of her life, but she's still able to find something good in it all. So, we can mope and feel guilty for the rest of our lives, or we can choose to be like Mrs. Li and be brave. Henry gave up his life-just like that without thinking twice; the least we can do for him is to move on and live a good life, don't you think?"

Tears continued to flow ever so freely down Mika's face. I let her mourn in silence as I too settled back on the bed and grieved for a great man. Everything had happened so quickly and without warning, we all needed time to adjust. While it wasn't fair and it wasn't right, life still went on- in rain or shine. And if Mrs. Li was able to smile through her tragedy, then we should also be able to shine a bright light in Henry's honour so that his death wasn't chosen in vain.

*

True to his wife's promise, Henry's service was held a few days later. While the man was never an international figure, nor had any parks or buildings named in his honour, he had made many friends through the years and was magnificent in their eyes as they all paid tribute to him. Tears were shed as stories were shared about Henry; and it didn't take long before the ceremony turned into a celebration of his great life. In a way, it was a joyous occasion and something that Henry would have wanted as a final farewell to his family and friends.

Mrs. Li held her head up high the entire day. She never once cried, but beamed with pride as people described what a great man her husband was. And as we all saw her stand beside Henry for the last time before his casket was carefully lowered to the ground, it was only then did she sink her head in remembrance of someone who had dedicated his life to her. The ceremony officially ended, but not before Mrs. Li could whisper lovingly to the man she ever loved, "I see you later, old man." It was enough to break your heart.

Grave melancholy hovered over us and especially so once we got home. When Aunt May passed, while there was sadness, there was also a sense of closure to her leaving so that when she was truly gone, we were able to find peace. But with Henry, finding closure to his passing was proving to be a more daunting task. We were given time to say our good-byes to

Aunt May and knew she had put up a good fight. But for Henry, his leaving was senseless, and without good reason. It felt as though he was never even given a fighting chance before being taken away. And it was now up to us, the people he had no choice but to leave behind, to make sense of it all.

Once at home, we each took a moment in our own way to soak in what had unfolded in these past few days. We all watched Mrs. Li walk back to a room she no longer shared with a husband and close the door softly behind her. Without a word, Mika also went back to her room leaving only Nancy and I.

From finding back hope to mourning someone who traded in his life to save mine- it was all too overwhelming. I suddenly needed air and dashed out to the balcony in need of some kind of miracle. As I raised my head and stared up into a blanket of darkness, I heard footsteps behind me and turned to find Nancy. Once again, she was by my side, supporting me in times of sorrow and despair.

Offering a weak but comforting smile, Nancy reached up and touched my arm delicately asking, "How are you holding up?"

Struggling to return her smile, I replied, "Alright I suppose. Think we've all been better though."

Nodding, Nancy followed my gaze, looking out over the balcony and took in a deep breath herself sighing, "A lot's happened, that's for sure. It's never easy saying good-bye, let alone to someone who saved your life and you didn't even get the chance to say thank-you...seems cruel and unfair to me."

Though I agreed, I could only manage a nod without saying anything. Staring ahead once more as though searching for answers, we remained quiet for awhile until I caught sight of Nancy standing beside me from the corner of my eye, and found myself stunned of her elegance and grace. Words could not describe how grateful I was for Henry to have saved her and Mika- the two people most precious in my life; and in that instance, I realized Henry had not only given me a second chance to live but also another chance to love. I couldn't waste anymore time with the woman I now knew I treasured more than life itself.

Without hesitation, I turned to Nancy and said, "Nancy, I don't want you to be my assistant anymore."

Startled and confused, she cocked her head to one side with a furrowed brow and asked, "What?"

"I know why you rejected me that night. I'd been thinking too much with my head like I always do with work and it made you feel like a commodity- which you're not. I should have told you this that night, but I panicked and said all the wrong things."

Still stunned, but pleasantly surprised, she replied, "Go on...I'm listening now."

I suddenly grew nervous and felt pink heat rise to my cheeks. But so much had already been wasted and lost, I was determined to not let Nancy go this time. Taking in a deep breath, I continued on making sure that every word I voiced came from the heart.

"I'm actually not logical at all. In fact, I'm quite an emotional person- so much sometimes I think it makes me a complete wreck. But working in the business that we're in, you have to learn to hide it and pretend you're anything but emotional. I've been so used pretending to be a rational person, I guess it's crippled me somewhat and I didn't even know it until now. I've never really thought about us...together...because you've always been with me and I had assumed it would be that way forever. I know that was selfish of me. It wasn't until I saw our photo that I smartened up and realized it's not a given that you've been with me all this time. It was your choice to stay, but I can't expect for you to be like this forever, it wouldn't be fair."

Taking in every word I said, Nancy replied, "Sounds pretty logical to me."

"No…that's what I'm trying to get at. For you to stay and be with me all this time was not logical; for me to feel the way that I do now is not logical." Standing directly in front of her, I made a bold move and held both her hands firmly in mine. "Nancy, I don't need anyone in my life to survive; but I don't just want to coast through life just to survive it. I want to live, and I know I won't be able to unless you're here with me to make me whole and show me that my life is worth something. It's always been you, Nancy and it has nothing to do with logic. After all this time, being with you comes naturally to me and I think it's the same for you too. It's the only explanation why you've always come first to mind when I'm happy and is always the first person I go to when I need help."

"So…you're basically saying I've turned into your emotional crutch…."

"No," I replied firmly. "It's the opposite. I've been thinking back to everything you've done for me Nancy and I want to be the person that you lean on for once. You can't tell me that in these past few months you haven't noticed a change in me. You've given me purpose and meaning and I want to be the person you run to when you're happy and sad."

Eyeing me cautiously, Nancy replied, "So…what now…?"

Before I could answer, there was a gentle tap of the glass door behind us and we instinctively dropped our hands. Turning around, we saw Mika smiling awkwardly as she slid open the door.

Embarrassed, but with a grin, she asked mischievously, "Oops...sorry...did I interrupt something?"

Knowing the moment was lost for now, I glanced at Nancy who was looking bashfully down at her feet, before saying, "Umm...it's alright...anything important?"

The tension was broken as we all relaxed and Mika answered, "Just that Mrs. Li cooked dinner and wants us to eat now."

We filed back into the dining room and took our seats. It was difficult not to look where Henry used to sit and feel sad all over again. Braving a smile, Mrs. Li shooed us to quickly eat, insisting that after a long day, we must all be hungry. *Bless the woman.*

Dinner was filled with talk of the service and how Henry would have been pleased of all that was arranged for him. Mrs. Li then went on naming people whom she knew would be great chauffeurs for me in place of Henry. "Good drivers!" she exclaimed. "My Henry still the best...but they are also very good."

Thankful for her recommendations, I told her hiring a replacement could wait a little longer. Whether it was out of respect for Henry or that I didn't trust another person behind the wheel of my cars, I simply just wasn't ready for anyone to take our Henry's place yet. I think it was something everyone around the table understood. Though we knew life would move on, we still needed more time to adjust and recalibrate the sudden loss in our lives.

As we finished the last morsel of food in our bowls, Mika announced, "I think I thought up a name for Capersville."

Excited to hear what she had thought of, I said, "Sure thing kid, shoot."

"How about 'The MayLi Community Centre'?" asked Mika hopefully.

As we all paused in thought, Nancy clapped her hands together and exclaimed excitedly, "It's a combination of your grandma's and Henry's names isn't? That's very thoughtful Mika."

Nodding her head excitedly, Mrs. Li chimed in, "Our Li name going to be famous…oohhh…the old man is going to be famous…he will be so happy in heaven!"

Chuckling, I nodded my head slowly as I thought out loud. "MayLi…MayLi Community Centre. It sounds unique and is definitely thoughtful. I'm going to have to run it by a few more people, but think it should work."

"And," added Nancy, "MayLi could also be a direct translation for beauty in Chinese. It's the perfect combination. Great thinking Mika."

As Mika beamed with pride, we all settled back in our seats and savoured the moment. It was indeed the perfect combination.

*

It was your typical day for a spectacular event. The sun was shining bright and strong against a clear blue sky with not a cloud in sight. The old Capersville building was finally remodeled, rebuilt….revitalized and was officially renamed 'The MayLi Community Centre'.

It was a very proud moment for many people. As speeches were made and the handshakes went around, there was finally closure. While there could never be an explanation for why such very important people so dear to us were snatched away so soon, having The MayLi Centre make its debut, standing ever so tall, pledged that Aunt May and Henry would always be around. Their names would forever be attached to something that would inspire and provide a helping hand to those less fortunate in a community they had called home.

There were many people invited to the grand opening of the centre and as I surveyed the crowd, I saw a group of youngsters laughing loudly with Mika as though sharing an inside joke. I figured they were some of Mika's classmates who had come celebrate her accomplishment. My eyes scanned her group of friends a little closer and saw that Steve was also among them having a good time with everyone. While Mika insisted they were still friends and nothing more, it was comforting to see the girl had finally found her sense of self. Mika's past had given her some precious life lessons that had ultimately help find her voice- and for that, I was grateful. Turning to leave the scene, I caught Mika's eye and as we nodded to each other from the distance, I was thrown off my feet with a snug heartwarming hug.

"Isaac- ah!" exclaimed Mrs. Li. "I dream yesterday that Henry and Aunt May so happy. You make them both famous you know?"

I laughed as I passed on the credit to everyone else who had a hand in the project. But Mrs. Li simply brushed it off and insisted that it was all my doing. Who was I to dispute a proud wife basking in her dear husband's glory today?

And at that moment, when nothing could have been more perfect, there was something still missing. Giving Mrs. Li one last hug, I made my way through the crowd searching for my own pride and joy. I found Nancy standing alone in the distance. As I approached her, she was still glowing with pride, awestruck of our masterpiece standing before us. I took her hand without fear and squeezed it ever so tightly. Without a word, she squeezed my hand back in return as we silently promised we would never let each other go. After all this time, I was finally a full and complete man coming home to his happiness.

Epilogue

The sun is setting and I finish reading Henry's inscription for the hundredth time. I can't help it. It's as though each time I read his writing, I am learning something new about him and life. For a man who never quite perfected his English, I'm not sure if he actually composed the inscription himself or simply copied it elsewhere. But it doesn't matter. They are still words he had chose and loved enough to record so that we wouldn't forget. It is still a piece of Henry- the man who gave up his life to save mine and the people I love. I am forever indebted to him.

But something is missing. The inscription is the only piece of writing in the book, and without thinking, I flip to the next page where it is blank, find a pen lying lifeless in the glove compartment and begin to write:

Dear Henry,

It has been six month since you've been gone. We have decided to start fresh by moving into a new place and begin a life that is without you. Though we know it can never be the same, we must try because that is something you would have wanted us to do. When movers came to pack away our things, I couldn't help but do an autopsy on my past life that was once grey and empty. I was chasing something that could never be captured and through it all, had let sadness haunt me.

I now know life can never fully encapsulate perfection, simply because people are flawed. But as imperfect as I am, I have managed to regain a life that has given me a purpose to find as much happiness as I can; making something that is perfect in my eyes.

Nancy and I have found love in each other and living well. Our rebellious Mika is no longer the wreck she once was. We see her challenge herself everyday to live a better life, leaving further behind a past that once snatched her faith and stole her innocence.

The moment you chose to sacrifice yourself, you gave all of us new life. So I ask you now to take my final blessing and let it carry you gently away in peace knowing we were given a second chance because you once lived.

Forever in your debt,

Isaac

P.S. Your wife loves and misses you dearly everyday

The End

Made in the USA
Charleston, SC
20 September 2012